ONE, TWO, THREE TIMES A MURDER

G.L. BARBOUR

ONE, TWO, THREE TIMES A MURDER

G.L. BARBOUR

ARPress LLC
45 Dan Road Suite 5
Canton MA 02021
Hotline: 1(888) 821-0229
Fax: 1(508) 545-7580

Ordering Information:
Quantity sales. Special discounts are available on quantity purchases by corporations, associations, and others. For details, contact the publisher at the address above.

Printed in the United States of America.

ISBN-13:   Softcover   979-8-89356-515-7
              Hardcover   979-8-89356-516-4
              eBook   979-8-89356-517-1

Library of Congress Control Number: 2024902567

Other Books by G. L. Barbour

Academic

Quality in the Veterans Health Administration

Redefining a Public Health System

Fiction

The Ron Looney Series

Death Unexpected

A Twisted Death

A Researched Death

Naked Death

Alibi for Death

Other

Montana in the Rearview Mirror

CONTENTS

Prologue

Thursday, June 20

The old man was clearly uncomfortable. He lay in the middle of a large bed in an even larger room, an intravenous line in his right arm. The high headboard behind him was carved in an ornate pattern that matched the richness of the room. To one side of the bed was a sitting area and on the other a fireplace with easy chairs; rich heavy drapes fell beside the windows that flanked the head of the bed. The old man looked small in the bed and even smaller in the room.

His breathing was obviously troubled; his breaths came quick and short and did not seem to move very much air. He clutched at the covers and coughed with a rattling sound; this movement stirred the nurse sitting beside the bed.

"Having trouble again?" she asked soothingly.

He nodded jerkily.

"Do you want me to call the doctor?"

Head shake.

"If you want I can put in the tube," as she said this she indicated the ventilator machine at the head of the bed. "Just like the doctor said, a little relaxation and you can get deep breaths again. I have all the medicines to do it right here."

"No. He . . . promised me," the old man croaked at her, unable to complete even short sentences.

"Yes. I know. But if you change your mind … "

"No damn … tubes . . . Morphine!"

"Of course. He left that for you, too." She turned to a small table nearby and opened the simple black case sitting there. She drew up some medication from a vial and slowly injected it into the intravenous line. As the medication took effect, the old man began to relax. His face sagged and he slumped back against his pillows. His breathing was no better but it no longer bothered him.

Later, as the waning afternoon sun sent its last rays through the windows, the doctor came into the room.

"I've given him the morphine several times. He's really running down." the nurse explained.

"Thank you, Elana. I'll stay with you for a while."

The next time the old man woke he had a spasm of coughing that caused a bubbling in his throat and panic in his eyes. The doctor stepped up to the side of the bed with morphine ready.

"No … tube … " came a faint plea.

"I know, friend. I promised. I'll help you be comfortable." As he was saying this the doctor injected the morphine. The man in the bed relaxed as the medicine effect took hold. A little later the shallow breathing became irregular and then stopped. The doctor waited a moment, then felt for a pulse and listened to the absent heart beat. He closed the man's eyelids and said, "I'll go notify the family."

The nurse turned to her final job, cleaning up the body, and said, "I haven't seen them today."

CHAPTER 1

Thursday, September 12

Ben Nealy was sitting at the nurses' station looking over the orders on a woman he had admitted two days ago. Ben was a third year medicine resident, PGY3 for short, on Ward 4C of New City Hospital, He had been thinking about his career decisions, first to choose a career in internal medicine and second to select New City for his training. Ben wanted to pursue an academic career and had been warned not to leave the University where he graduated. But New City was one of the developing types of hospitals training medical students and residents. Since the Second World War, most such training for academic careers had been accomplished in University hospitals and VA medical centers attached to a medical school. The advent of Medicare resulted in fewer patients being viewed as 'uninsured', however, and the patient population in those facilities decreased. A different way of training resident physicians, particularly for active practice rather than academia began to grow in popularity. This method utilized the patient load and the expertise of practicing physicians in private hospitals in nearly every city. New City was one of these sites. Initially serving Cincinnati as a Railway Hospital located near the tracks and the river, it was adopted by the city for a while until a local group bought the facility, changed the name, and pressed for significant improvements and, ultimately, the academic partnership with South West Ohio Medical School. Ben chose to do his residency at New City for several reasons. He liked the city, it gave him the exposure he thought appropriate for an academic career and his latest reason was he wanted to be near to Susan Chang, an emergency nurse in New City.

Ben felt he was learning both academic and practical medical information here at New City in the private setting because the attending physicians were all University appointed teachers and researchers. Now, in his third post-graduate year in the program, Ben had been involved in first-rate experiences and was comfortable working on the ward with his two interns. The inpatient teaching program at New City consisted of teams composed of two interns, or PGY-1 trainees, supervised daily by a third year resident and overseen by a board-certified internist faculty member as attending physician. Teams generally were responsible for 20-24 patients at a given moment and provided all care from admission to discharge. There also were subspecialty faculty and their trainees, fellows at the PGY4 or 5 level available for consultation, making the academic environment equivalent to any University setting.

Ben's beeper sounded and he recognized the number of the emergency room. Knowing that his team was 'up' for the next admission, he took a deep breath and decided to head to the emergency area right away rather than sending the responsible intern. He knew the interns' various patient loads and decided that, no matter the issue in emergency, Denis Albritton was going to be assigned the new case, not Allison Yamamoto. Both were bright and capable but Allison seemed to grasp the 'why' of things a little more quickly. Denis, not really a plodder, just took a little longer to evince second and third level understanding. But that wasn't bad since his third level was very complete, once he got there. Ben knew his job was to see that Denis became more proficient at getting to that deep level during his internship year. Ben had just returned to the ward from lunch and knew that Denis was in the physician workroom, so he walked there and stuck his head in the door.

"Hey, Denis. Let's go meet your new one down in the emergency area."

The stocky, thin-haired young man with round glasses looked up and commented, "Already? Crap, I'm not through writing up this set of orders from rounds this morning."

"You gotta get faster, my man. You have eight others to take care of and who knows what's waiting in the ED."

"Don't you know?"

"I'm going down to find out. Better get a move on. Never want to show up after your resident sees the patient, right?"

"Just let me enter these orders and I'll be right down." Denis turned back to the computer and tried to find his place in the orders.

"Not waiting," Ben said as he headed for the elevators. He had a brisk manner about him in virtually all things. He thought fast, ate fast and walked even faster, and he made it to the elevators while Denis was still typing digitized orders into the system.

Ben's blond hair was cut in the style common for that day, medium on the sides, longer on top, and sticking up. He wore the usual uniform of a PGY3: khakis, a button-down blue oxford-shirt with the long sleeves rolled up to mid forearm, and New Balance deck shoes without socks. Ben's father, owner and operator of a building supply business in Kentucky, frequently looked at his son's wardrobe and said, "You forgot to wear any socks," in the slow drawl of Terry Bradshaw telling the sushi chef, "You forgot to cook this." His father thought this was amusing, and perhaps it was for the first dozen times.

On the first floor, Ben skirted the lobby to the rear of the hospital and took the hall to the backend of the ED. As he entered, the clerk looked up. "Well, if it ain't Super Ben, come to help us all out!"

"Carla, you're the only one that calls me that and you know I'd come in a heartbeat anytime you call." Ben winked at the black-haired middle-aged woman behind the desk

"Yeah, well, you waited till there was an admission for you."

"I was saving lives upstairs."

"Is that your new superpower?"

"Nope. Same old one. What's this new patient?"

"Really an old one. But you can get the skinny from Betty. They're all down in Three."

Ben started down the hallway and half-turned back toward Carla and requested, "Would you please send Denis down there whenever he shows up?" She nodded assent and he continued on.

Room Three was full of people when he got there. Ben quickly sized up them up as wife and two adult children gathered around the new patient in the bed. Somewhat puzzling was the presence of three medical professionals, two nurses and the ED physician, Betty Wilcox, a friend and mentor for Ben. As Ben entered the small examining room, the nurses subtly moved a step back to give him room. He raised his eyebrows questioningly at Wilcox.

"Dr. Nealy, this is Mr. Grover Kinney, who was recently discharged from here but is having recurrent symptoms," Wilcox said with an overly formal air. "I'm going to admit him to you for evaluation and treatment."

Ben immediately fell into the pageantry. "Thank you, Dr. Wilcox. Let me have a moment and I'll be right along." He nodded to her and she and the nurses left the room. Ben stepped to the patient's right side and extended his hand. "Mr. Kinney, I'm Dr. Nealy, and I'll be caring for you when you get upstairs. Is there anything you need right now?"

The patient said softly, "No. I just want you get to the bottom of this damned pain and vomiting."

"Are you having pain now?"

"No. But it's gonna come back. Always does."

"All right, sir. Let me get some paperwork done so we can get you moved upstairs." Turning to the wife he asked," Mrs. Kinney? And are these your children?" he said, nodding at each of the family members.

"This is Anna and Chad," Mrs. Kinney said. "They wanted to come and make sure things were going OK for him." Ben smiled and nodded at the two noticing that their faces were dour and both had their arms crossed. They nodded at his recognition but it seemed rather perfunctory.

"I understand. And I'm glad you came. There will be another doctor coming down to see you. His name is Dr. Albritton. He and I will be your doctors on the ward upstairs. Again, do you need anything right now?"

"Nope. Let's get started on finding out what's going on." Mr. Kinney moaned. His words were accompanied by a small grimace as he tried to get comfortable in the bed.

"Exactly. Just let me pop out and get the paperwork going."

Ben left the room quietly sliding the glass door closed, stepped to the ward clerk's desk and said, "Let's put him on my ward. I think we have a couple of empty beds." Knowing that an order for admission would have to come from Dr. Wilcox, Ben went off in search of her. He found her with one of the nurses in the work area right behind the nurses' station.

"So, Betty, this is a funny story, huh?"

"Hey Ben. One without much in the way of laughs." Betty Wilcox had been one of Ben's favorite mentors in the teaching program and their interaction had always been warm.

"OK. Could we grab a cup of coffee while you tell me about it?"

When they finally sat in the doctors' work area with their fresh cups of coffee, Betty Wilcox let out a sigh. "I'm really sorry about this, Ben. This guy, Kinney, was here on 3B back in the summer. Stayed almost three weeks without a diagnosis."

"And why's he back?" Ben asked, his curiosity aroused. In most training hospitals, patients who are readmitted with complaints similar to their last admission were commonly returned to the care of their previous team. The rationale for this practice was if something could be learned that was missed the first time, the original team would be best positioned to recognize what that was. Betty's mention of the previous admission 'in the summer' however, meant that the ward team that previously cared for Mr. Kinney would now have rotated to other responsibilities. Such rotations occurred every two months throughout the academic year in order to give trainees the widest possible experience. No matter where Mr. Kinney was admitted, he would have a new set of physicians, attending, resident and intern.

"He came in back then with unexplained weight loss. About twenty-five pounds." Betty explained with a sigh. "Associated with stomach pain and vomiting. Apparently he had all the usual workup, GI series, CT scan, complete metabolic panel—and zippo, nothing. Mild anemia but nothing else. And after about a week, he got hungry and started to eat. His pain vanished and suddenly they noticed he'd gained about five pounds. So there they were with no findings and a patient with no symptoms." Betty shook her head and looked into her cup. "So, he went home-without a diagnosis. I mean if you consider that 'abdominal pain and weight loss' are not diagnoses."

"Which they are not."

"Now he says he was fine at home for about a month, and then the pain and vomiting started up again, and he's lost all the weight he gained."

"You got any ideas about this pain?" Ben wondered if the astute ED physician might have some new insight into Kinney's problem.

"Not really. Belly is soft, bowel sounds are present. No organomegaly, and the labs are all just like before. Mild anemia and that's it."

"So why were you so formal in there?" Ben inquired in an off-hand way as he took a swallow of coffee.

"I don't know. The family dynamic just seemed off. The kids act like they don't believe he's really having pain." Ben remembered the feeling he had of the children being distant from the wife's concern about Mr. Kinney. "I thought they were sorta disconnected," he added.

"It just felt chilly in there and I wasn't comfortable being all cheery," Betty explained. Ben nodded with understanding.

"What's he do?"

"Farmer. Small farm just north of here. Apparently it's just the two of them. I think the kids are out of the house. They look old enough."

"Well water?"

"Look, I didn't take a public health history, so don't go all John Snow on me," she said smiling at him and referring to the famous public health researcher in the mid 19th century who uncovered the cause for a cholera epidemic in London. "I told you what I've got, and that's it."

"OK. We got it from here. Want me to tell you when we find out?"

"I don't care. Just as long as he doesn't come back in here."

Ben went back to Room 3 and found Denis already involved in taking a thorough history, so he told Mr. Kinney he would see him upstairs and left.

On rounds that morning, Ben and the attending physician, George Hacker, had made some suggestions to Denis and the other intern that needed following up on. Ben took himself to the physician workroom on the ward, opened up the electronic record on Grover Kinney's last admission, and started reading.

CHAPTER 2

Thursday, September 12

After thirty minutes of review with Mr. Kinney's electronic medical record, Ben felt he had some idea of the diagnostic process that occurred during the previous admission. Because the complaints were gastrointestinal all the initial studies focused on the stomach. And, just as Betty had told him, all the results were normal. Except for some mild gastritis seen on endoscopy, everything about Mr. Kinney's GI tract seemed perfectly normal.

And most of the laboratory values were also not helpful. Ben noted the mild anemia mentioned before and thought that was all there was to that. Until he noticed something else a little odd about the automated blood counts. The previous team had checked the blood counts several times during the hospital stay to be certain that the anemia was not worsening. Every one of those examinations was a complete blood count or CBC and included the results of Mr. Kinney's white blood cells as well as the red cells involved in the anemia. Every one of the CBC reports noted that the white blood cell count was slightly elevated something that commonly indicates an infection. But Ben's review of the progress notes found no mention of this finding by the team.

And he found it very difficult to find much of anything noted by the team during that stay because of the length of the chart. Like many physicians reviewing a medical record, Ben wanted to follow the thinking of the treating physicians and so he initially focused on the doctors' progress notes. And what he found was the now familiar problem of trying to find the needle in a haystack. Medicaid and other federal funding requirements demanded that any physician's note for a given hospital day must contain information indicating awareness of all other professionals' input, laboratory values, and radiographic findings up to that time. Individuals making such requirements apparently assumed every physician was afflicted with short-term memory loss and could not possibly remember what happened yesterday without writing it down and doing so every day. Of course, with the electronic record, one did not have to actually write anything-it was embarrassingly simple to cut and paste so that you also didn't have to read anything. The net result was an enormous volume of notes, each containing all the preceding information, sparse new information, and in the case of interns' notes, an assessment that often remained the same from day to day.

Ben was also a reader of the nurses' notes. He knew that those notes were not cluttered with redundancy and often gave a better perspective on patient status. In Mr. Kinney's chart, however, even the nurses daily annotations simply showed the slow improvement from admission to discharge without explanation.

He was interrupted during his reading a couple of times by the nurses asking about the admission and once he left the room to greet Mr. Kinney and cohort as he was brought to the ward and placed in a bed. Later. after spending a total of nearly two hours with the chart, Ben got up from his chair and stretched. He was not pleased with his review of Grover Kinney's medical record from July. The testing sequences did not suggest pathology and the intern's progress notes were less than helpful

Frustrated with his review of the record, Ben found Mr. Kinney's room and sat down next to the bed to take a history himself. Kinney noted that he had said it all several times before, but Ben persisted, explaining that each physician needed to hear the pertinent facts individually. He knew that every physician asks even similar questions-and follow-up-with enough difference that new information is commonly uncovered. That was not the case, this time, however.

Forty-five minutes later, he went back to the physician workroom and found Denis just completing his admitting orders. They reviewed the orders quickly and Denis asked what Ben had learned from his examination of Kinney.

"I don't think I got any information that wasn't commented on by you and the previous team at least three times," he admitted. "But there was something in the old record that I'm wondering about."

"What's that?'

"Every CBC had a slightly elevated white count."

"What's that about?" Denis queried.

"That's what we gotta figure out, my man. Did I ever tell you about my rotation last year on Hematology?"

"Some things."

"Dr. Franco had me study every consult we saw by starting with the peripheral blood smear. His rule was I needed to look at over 100 fields on the slide before I saw the patient."

"Really? What for?"

"He said my history and physical would be much better focused and thorough if I knew what the peripheral smear showed."

"Huh. I've never heard that before."

"I hadn't either, but it turned out to be true more often that not. For instance, if the patient has anemia, Franco said you could figure out the cause about 75 percent of the time by looking at the red cells. Pale, small cells are due to iron deficiency and the major cause of iron deficiency is, what, Denis?"

"Uh, blood loss?"

"Right. And the most common cause of blood loss is?

"Bleeding?"

"From"

"GI?"

"Exactly. Unless the patient is a woman with heavy menstrual periods."

'How's that gonna help us with Kinney?"

"Don't know. That's why we're on our way to the lab."

They went to the pathology laboratory in the hospital basement, where they began in the chemistry section. One of the technicians got them the most recent set of values measured on Mr. Kinney, which had been obtained in the emergency area earlier in the day._Those numbers were remarkably normal, as Betty Wilcox had said. Whatever the chronic illness Mr. Kinney had, it was not disturbing his internal chemistry. After a brief chat about the normality of the numbers the two doctors moved to the hematology section.

Ben asked the chief technician to help him find the peripheral blood smear for Grover Kinney. That took a few minutes and while the search was ongoing Ben said to Denis, "Franco taught me how to estimate the platelet count for a patient by looking at the peripheral smear."

"Are you any good at it?"

"Usually within 25 thousand, out of 200-300 thousand."

"That's pretty good. Can you teach me to do that?"

"If we have a couple hundred slides and all the time in the world."

When the technician handed Ben the slide he had requested, he took Denis over to the multiheaded teaching microscope and put the slide in place. Over the next few minutes Ben quizzed Denis about the number of platelets in a given field and asked him to closely examine the various white cells. He pointed out some of the features of these cells, including that there were some dark blue colored white cells.

"Yeah, those are basophiles," Denis said. "I know that."

"Did you know that basophiles are the most fragile of the white cells?"

"No. So what?"

'Well if you look at a smear and don't see basophiles, the slide was poorly made and you should not base much on it."

"Oh." Denis looked more intently into the microscope to examine these fragile cells.

"Now look at the red cells. What do you see?"

"They're normal sized and I think that's normal color."

"Meaning?"

"Probably not iron deficiency. More like a bone marrow production issue." Denis was beginning to feel more confident in his interpretation.

"Very good. What else?"

"I don't see a lot of broken cells."

"I don't either. What about these two over here?" Ben indicated some cells toward the periphery using the light pointer in the microscope.

"I don't know, what?"

"Do they look like all the others?"

"No," said Denis a little defensively. "They do have something on them."

"Really? Is it 'on' them or 'in' them?

"I can't tell."

"Do you see that stuff anywhere other than 'on' the red cells?

Denis was quiet for a minute or two while he dialed around the slide before saying, "No. It's always on the red cells. And there's several like that."

"Yep." Ben said pulling away from the microscope. "And I would like a second opinion about that." He called to the technician and asked whether Dr. Song was around. Ben had benefitted from the teaching experiences in Dr. Song's autopsy room and was one of her biggest fans in the teaching program.

Monique Song, Chief of the Anatomical Laboratory happened to be in her office and responded to the request for consultation. She came to the microscope and indicated that she wanted to look at the smear before being told anything about the patient. Monique spent less than two minutes looking at the smear alone and then indicated that Ben and Denis were to join her. She pointed out a couple of things to them and then settled on the red cells with the 'stuff in them'. She turned to Denis and asked, "What do you see?"

"Some blue stuff like it's on the red cells."

"It's in the red cells. What is that?"

"I don't know."

Monique looked at Ben. "Is this your question?"

"It is. I think it's basophilic stippling. But I've only seen that once before and I'd like to be sure."

"Well, you're absolutely correct. That is fairly classic basophilic stippling. You know such findings often don't show up on the automated counter-the machines interpret those as white cells. Pretty clever of you, Dr. Nealy. What do you think is going on?"

Ben said, "I didn't know that bit about the counter calling them white cells. That explains the elevated white count. Denis, what does this mean for our patient?" Ben again wanted to press his charge to make a diagnosis.

Denis was unsure and hesitatingly offered, "I'm not sure what that means. I remember something about that but it escapes me now."

"Well," Dr. Song explained, "it usually means that the production of red cells in the bone marrow has been disrupted by some toxin, usually a heavy metal like … "

"Lead!" cried Denis. "I remember now. It's a sign of lead poisoning. And this guy's got it. Oh man, what a scoop!"

"Yes," smiled Monique, "that's will be quite the scoop. Now let's prove it with a blood and urine lead level."

CHAPTER 3

Friday, September 13

om Bolling was driving to work at New City Hospital in his
truck. Tom liked his ride, the Ford F-150, with a standard cab,
split bench seats and ample legroom so that he felt comfortably away
from the traffic that surrounded him on the way in. Plus, he liked the
height of the truck that put him a decent distance above the rest of
the commuting traffic around Cincinnati. Tom had always thought of
himself as one who looked 'far ahead' and the increased vision in the
truck fit his image and his psyche. Tom Bolling was a retired brigadier
general from the U.S. Air Force medical service corps. An orthopedic
surgeon with combat zone experience, he had retired before adding
another star in order to bring some stability to his life. He had taken
the position as chief of staff at the New City Hospital in Cincinnati a
few years ago and he and Sandra had nicely settled in to civilian life.
Except, of course, that nothing about his new life and new position
was 'settled'.

The upscale image of the New City's current academic program
that had appealed to Tom was largely reflected in building programs
from the late 1990s; gleaming exterior finish with soaring columns
and arching entrances. Those who worked there knew that those
structures were abutted against blocky renovations created by the city
planners in the 1950s and that those improvements were stitched to

the original Railway building, five stories high, red brick and only fifty feet wide built in 1910. That building was now high-rent office space for specialists practicing in New City. The mix of architecture from the different decades was internally mirrored by the attitudes of some practitioners. Tom's predecessor as chief of staff had not been able to meld the private practice physicians and faculty physicians hired for the affiliation to do teaching into a cohesive group. Tom was also finding unanticipated travails in attempting that same job. And it wasn't only issues of clinical care or problems with the physician component of the hospital that created headaches for him.

Every day now started with a morning meeting with Sam Mastone, the hospital director, who wanted to know too many details about how things worked on the clinical side of the hospital. Sam was a former personnel officer and he tended to see things as entries in a Personnel Folder-with no gray shades possible. To Sam, everything was black or white, it was good for the hospital or not. And, clearly, what was good for the hospital was, in Sam's mind, also good for Sam Mastone. That perspective created a micro-management attitude that Tom found initially just annoying but which after a few years had become a constant irritant and a growing dissatisfier with his job.

Mastone's morning meeting was a perfect place for Sam's micro-management to manifest itself. The meeting involved only a few of the executives at New City, specifically Sam, the director, Allen, the assistant director, Tom and Roslyn Burke, the chief nurse at New City. Further, each of the executives brought their primary assistant to the meeting. Mastone's reason for the meeting was to keep the executives aware of issues that needed immediate attention. Tom knew that the military had such meetings as well but they were run very differently. In the Air Force, no one raised an issue that fell in their responsibility unless they needed assistance in resolving the matter. In Mastone's meeting, issues were brought up, in Tom's opinion, just so some people could talk. Problems that cut across disciplines were usually talked about a great deal before someone-often someone not in the room-was identified as the individual to resolve the issue. And, more often than not, Mastone's micro-management style was to dictate the parameters around which the issue was to be solved by that other person.

Fortunately for him, Tom's wife, Sandra, was able to convince him to find ways of dealing with Sam that didn't involve either giving in to his micro style or resigning from the chief of staff role. Sandra's point was that everyone knew how Sam was and almost everyone had adopted a means of living with the man and his ways. Somehow virtually all employees of New City who had to interact with the Director on a regular basis had come to the realization that he wasn't about to change, so they did.

At one point, early in his tenure at New City, Tom had mused about a plan that he had hatched that he believed would get Sam to change and become a better manager and leader. Sandra listened to the entire plan without much comment until Tom finally said, "what do you think, honey?" Her response was to ask, Tom to consider just one other thing.

"Look," she said, "He is a career employee of the system, He has had several responsible jobs, Personnel Officer, Assistant Director and now Director of a large tertiary care academic hospital. He has gotten praise and raises and is now on top of the heap. Can you tell me what's not working for him?"

Tom thought about this insight and was reminded about the old adage about how many psychiatrists it takes to change a light bulb-only one, but the light bulb has to really want to change. He realized that his plan to change Sam was doomed because the man didn't want to change and had no motivation to change. So Tom began to work on himself to change his response to Sam. He knew he personally was ill-suited to do the 'water off a duck's back' approach so he decided he would adopt a principal he knew from the Air Force. When an officer, especially one new to the command, tried to make disruptive changes in the system, the non-commissioned officers under that officer played the 'work to rule' game to its fullest. Every possible barrier, additional piece of paperwork and delay tactic that could be brought to bear was employed until the officer, usually beset by many other more pressing issues, just let his or her idea of change die on the vine. Tom had made that work several times with Sam and other times he developed a business plan to show that immediate change was not necessary. The result of using these tactics was that Sam was slowly becoming more open to listening to Tom's opinion rather than needing a formal study to convince him to listen.

Nonetheless, Tom had other issues to face that had nothing to do with Sam. First was the recent set of vacancies in the Cardiology Division. This division was among the leaders in the income streams of the hospital and the vacancies were costing the hospital. The lack of salary outlay for the positions was not a real savings when one counted the loss of income those physicians and their procedures could bring in. Tom had asked the Division to help him determine the direction of recruiting-emphasis on research or clinical activity-and they were to give him their recommendation very soon. He knew his approach to drumming up some candidates would be different for the two; he also realized that their academic partner at the University saw the New City Cardiology Division as predominantly clinical teachers rather than researchers and he expected the recommendation to support that. Plus, he didn't really want to be recruiting at that level.

In addition, Tom was planning a better push for getting the employees to get their flu shots this year. Last year only about 72% of the staff and employee base had done so and when the vaccine turned out to only be about 10% effective when the viral strain mutated, the hospital had difficulty maintaining a full work force in many areas while nurses, technicians and others were out sick. Tom was toying with an idea of having an all-employee presentation of the need for vaccination and then letting everyone watch as he and Sam and all the other Division leaders stepped up and got their vaccination. Of course, he was going to have to wrestle a number of people into his way of thinking to bring that to reality.

And, not completely in the back of his mind, Tom was tinkering with plans for a presentation he had been asked to make-almost like a

Grand Rounds-to the orthopedic faculty, staff and residents about the Fast Track approach he had developed and implemented at Balad for blast injuries to the lower extremity.

As usual, Tom spent an inadequate amount of time thinking on each of these issues during his drive to the hospital so that, as he turned into the parking garage and pulled out his access card, he had no answers to anything and it was now time to start another day which he knew would only add problems to his list of concerns.

CHAPTER 4

Friday, September 13

After parking in his reserved spot, Tom walked into the lobby and caught the eye of his favorite barista, Nick, at the Green Bean coffee kiosk in the lobby. Nick was also an Air Force veteran and he and Tom shared some common memories. Shortly after Tom arrived at New City and came to the Green Bean for coffee, Nick had introduced himself and talked with Tom about how he would like his coffee. They finally decided that Tom's 'usual' would henceforth be a Black Eye Americano-two espresso shots in a cup of black coffee. As he stood at the far end of the kiosk after paying for his drink, Tom thought 'This is a day I am likely to need more than one of these Black Eyes before I get home.'

Fifteen minutes later he was still working on that first one as he entered the conference room for the morning meeting. He had talked to Mary Brighthouse, his secretary and confirmed some meetings for the day and heard briefly from his Executive Assistant, Beverly Hancock about the overnight statistics and knew there were no major problems. Over the years he had coaxed Sam not to spend time in the morning meeting going over the bed occupancy rate or the outpatient clinic times as long as they fell within a specified range of 'acceptable'.

For more than a year the focus of the morning meeting had slowly shifted, at Tom's perseverance to issues of real importance.

They discussed deaths, major incidents and questions that cut across disciplines. Tom had not yet been successful, however, in getting the assignment of responsibility to be placed on the executives rather than an absent individual. Even more frustrating to Tom, Sam continued to insist that he personally provide all the requisite steps for problem resolution. Nonetheless Tom felt he was gaining ground largely by applying Susan's wise advice.

Tom smiled at the chief nurse, Roslyn Burke and her executive officer, Alena Preston and got a tentative nod from each of them in return. As he took his seat to the right of Mastone's chair, Tom noted that Nancy Hawes, the nurse who headed up the utilization review program was also at the table and he had a passing qualm that an unexpected shoe was going to drop. Beverly sat on Tom's right and they exchanged looks about Nancy's presence.

Promptly at eight o'clock, Sam Mastone bustled in from his adjoining office and took his chair at the head of the table, smiled unconvincingly around the table and opened the meeting; "I see there were no problems last night." He was not a tall man and slightly thick around the middle like one who enjoyed his pasta. His dark slicked down hair and a complexion of pale olive completed the picture of a Mafioso don. He always wore dark, pinstriped suits and rarely smiled. In his usual custom, Sam began by looking at the paper reports of the previous 24 hours of activity. Everyone knew he had these reports on his desk at seven o'clock and that he had surely read them before coming to the meeting. Nonetheless they all kept up the façade and waited for him to look up and start the reporting. When he did, each person dutifully noted their agreement with the assessment that 'nothing big had happened."

When discussion got around to Roslyn, she introduced Nancy and her topic for discussion by saying, "Nancy has been looking at some of the Utilization Review data and has some very interesting issues to bring up." She nodded to Nancy as an assent to begin her presentation.

"As Ms. Burke said, I have been looking closely at a particular data set in the utilization management office. We collect this information usually for quarterly reporting but something in the numbers stood out a little over a month ago. After I discussed it with Ms Burke we decided it should be presented to the executive meeting."

Tom thought, 'Is this going to be a blindside from Nursing?'

Nancy went on, "As everyone knows we regularly review admissions against guidelines for funding purposes. When our patients do not meet the criteria for admission Medicare and most insurance agencies deny us payment for their inpatient care." She paused and looked around.

"Since July we have had a significant number of admissions from the interns' clinics that are not appropriate and . . ."

"Help me understand here," Tom interrupted. "What is 'inappropriate'?"

"I mean the admissions don't meet criteria for admission."

"Explain that to me, please."

"Well, you know we are using the InterQual criteria to determine appropriateness of admissions and care, right?" Tom signified his knowledge of this fact. Nancy went on, "National statistics indicate that about 4 percent of all admissions to general medical or surgical beds do not meet these criteria and should not have been admitted ... "

"Hang on," said Tom. "I'm familiar with InterQual. I worked on some of the VA-DoD guidelines and I know these commercial ones are similar. They are guidelines, not absolute criteria. Nobody carved these in stone."

"Even so, doctor, our patient mix is mostly private insurance now but we still have a fair amount of Medicare and Medicaid patients and both the government and the insurers are using these criteria to question admissions that they consider inappropriate and refusing to pay. It appears that our educational program is costing us more than just the stipends for the interns."

"How much?"

"Approximately $40,000 since July. I started noticing the trend late that month and have been collecting data since."

Sam broke in, "Why didn't I know about this sooner?"

Tom jumped in to the conversation to avoid some detailed discussion about accounting and said, "This is the first I've heard of this, too, Sam. But it's clearly important and my responsibility. I'll handle it."

Sam seemed to ponder the possibility of there being a significant problem in the hospital and him not telling someone how to fix it. Then he relented, nodded sternly toward Tom and said, "Alright, then."

The nursing executives nodded vigorously at this, suppressing outright smiles. Sam was about to say something else when Tom went on, "Nancy, could you let me have the data you have?"

As she passed a large manila folder across the table, Tom turned to Sam and said, "I'll get back to you when I have digested these data."

And the meeting ended on that note.

In the hallway on the way to their offices, Tom handed the manila folder to Beverly and said, "Give me your opinion. Soon." After another step he added, "Please."

CHAPTER 5

Saturday, September 14

Teaching rounds with the attending physician, resident, and interns were held regularly on Monday, Wednesday and Friday mornings and commonly extended to the lunch hour. Saturday morning rounds were more focused on getting things done and were usually short and this was no exception. The attending, George Hacker, was aware of everything going on with the patients on the ward and there were no big changes over the night; rounds were completed well before 11:00 and Denis and Allison grabbed some coffee and sat down to finish chart work before heading home. Ben was wondering whether he could get Susan to leave the ED for lunch with him in the cafeteria when he remembered that Denis didn't mention a report on the lead level in Kinney's urine.

He opened the electronic record and started through the lab values and realized why no report had been made-there was no result in the record. As he sat there wondering how long it would take for the urine lead level to be measured, the lab page automatically refreshed in front of him. And there was the lab report: urine lead was zero. Not even trace. "Bummer," he thought. "I really hoped we had the answer. Wonder if there's a way his urine lead level could be low and him still have lead poisoning?"

Ben decided to check and see whether his attending was still in the building for a quick consult. He walked down a flight of stairs and took the flyover into the old Railway medical office building to where Hacker had his office. Sure enough, Hacker was sitting in his office writing up a case report. "Can't get stuff like this done at home," he said. "Kids are all over the house."

"Maybe you have too many kids," Ben offered.

"Not really. I'd have more but my wife says I'd need another wife."

"I hear you."

"So, why are you over here? Something go sour on the ward?"

Ben sat down in front of Hacker's desk. "I need a quick answer. I could go to the library or spend the afternoon on PubMed but I think you can set me straight."

"Shoot."

"Is there any way this guy, Kinney, could have lead poisoning and not have lead in his urine? His value is zero, by the way."

"Zero? That's actually pretty low. But your question is: 'could he have systemic poisoning-gut and bone marrow-without spilling in the urine? Right?"

"That's about it."

"Well, lead competes with calcium in the body so over time it is sunk into bone and we don't see elevated levels in the blood-so at that time I'm pretty sure the urine level would be low also … but maybe not zero."

"And that takes some time, right?" said Ben, shaking his head. "This guy was having symptoms until three days ago."

"Here's a thought," said Hacker. "Maybe it's not lead? Maybe the stippling misled us. Seems like lead is out of the picture, acutely at least. What are other things that can cause stippling?"

"That's why I came over here. I wanted some guidance."

"Well, I think you can see it post-splenectomy."

"He still has his spleen."

"Thalassemia? Sickle Cell?"

"Doesn't fit the picture."

"Well," said Hatcher, "seems the one thing we do know is that it is not lead poisoning."

"Yeah, I guess so," Ben said dispiritedly. "I was really hoping … "

Hacker looked at him for along moment and then said, "Did I ever tell you about trading patients?"

"Don't think so. Doesn't sound familiar."

"When I was a resident on the wards a couple of times I was just stumped about a patient; could not figure out what was going on with them and was really spinning my wheels. So, I walked over to the other side and traded that patient for a similar one with another resident."

"Here? At New City?"

"Actually, no. We were at the VA. But we were both stuck, probably something like forest and trees, I guess. So we swapped. And within a few days each of us had figured out the other's problem. Made a diagnosis. Effected a cure."

"Are you trying to get Kinney off our service?" Ben was grinning because he knew where Hacker was going with this story.

"Of course not. You'll figure it out. You just have to be someone else to do it," Hacker said leaning back and putting his hands on his head.

Ben laughed and left the office. On the way back to the ward he considered several ways to approach the issue that would implement the recommendation he got from Hacker. And he settled on the most obvious one.

When he arrived back on the ward, he went immediately to Mr. Kinney's room. There were no visitors and Kinney had just finished his lunch. Noting that was the first time the patient had eaten a meal since admission, Ben thought, 'This is the right time for this new approach.' He had decided to be someone other than a supervising resident; he would be the intern for this patient.

He moved the luncheon tray out of the way, stuck out his hand and said, "Hello, Mr. Kinney. My name is Ben Nealy. I'm one of the doctors here on the ward and I want to talk to you about why you have come into the hospital."

Kinney looked at him with tilted head and said slowly, "Oh … K."

Ben smiled at him. "I know we have met before but I'm going to be someone else right now." And he started all over with, "Can you tell me what's been bothering you?"

Twenty minutes later, Ben started a complete physical exam on Kinney, as if he had never seen him before. Took his blood pressure, listened to his lungs, looked in his eyes and examined him for lymph nodes. As he was examining Kinney's arms and hands he turned the hands over and looked at the fingernails.

"Mr. Kinney, what kind of farmer are you?"

"Small. Kinda like truck farming. I grow vegetables for local restaurants, you know. Tomatoes, onions, lettuce, cabbage. Tried strawberries but couldn't make 'em work."

"Mr. Kinney, I see some discoloration on your fingernails. I don't think I saw that before. Is it new?"

"Huh. Yeah. I don't think I had anything like that before. What's that mean?"

"Well, I'm not completely sure either. But I'm gonna find out."

Later, Ben sat down in the doctors work room and typed in his new physical examination results and ordered new blood and urine tests. He finished all this work and leaned back, feeling very proud of himself. Then he remembered he had missed lunch but decided to go to the ED and see Susan anyway.

CHAPTER 6

Monday September 16

Tom had asked Beverly to review the work done by Nancy for several reasons. Not the least of those reasons was the high regard he had for her analytic capability and thoughtfulness. Bev was his major asset in adjusting to the vicissitudes of New City, an ally that was not a physician and who always brought the non-medical aspect of issues and solutions to the fore. She was essential to his attempts at making performance improvements throughout the hospital, often mirroring the comments and observations that Sandra made about personalities and using the calendar to better advantage. Bev had been around New City for several years before Tom arrived and had experience and insight into historical decisions that helped him to better understand how to approach issues.

At the morning meeting she told Tom she would have her analysis ready in an hour or so and she had just now finished organizing the different patterns she had identified. She had promised Tom, or 'Dr. Bolling' as she always referred to him in public, that she would brief him this morning about the data Nancy Hawes had brought to their attention. She said she had used Friday afternoon to put the information into a friendlier spreadsheet arrangement and spent some time on Saturday afternoon running some analytics.

Tom could hear her printer start up in her office next to his and anticipated that she would be flexing her neck, stretching her arms and packing up materials for her presentation. Sometimes he thought she was a little obsessive about some details but had learned that when he tried to explain things to Mastone, Bev's details turned out to be essential.

When her knock on the door came, he looked up from his email and smiled. "Come on in. I'm ready for enlightenment."

"Well, the light has already been turned on this issue," Bev said, sitting in the chair beside the desk and handing him the printouts. "But we may be able to move it around a little and shine it in the shadows."

Thirty minutes later, Tom was thoroughly briefed on the data that Nancy had collected and the supplemental information that Bev was able to extract from the medical records. At the most superficial level, Nancy's assessment was absolutely correct-comparison of the individual patient's clinical findings at the time they were admitted compared to the criteria in the utilization review criteria indicated that slightly more than 12 percent of the admissions to hospital from the interns' clinic since July 1 did not meet the standard for admission to an acute level bed. The patients were not sick enough to be in a hospital according to the criteria.

But Beverly had not stopped with that piece of reckoning. She knew how Tom thought and how his simple questions of "why?" and "how do you know that?" always drove conversations into territory that was generally unexpected by others and which often led to surprising answers. So she had done additional digging and began to put out that information in small packets. "Interestingly, about a third of the admissions didn't really have a diagnosis," she noted.

"What? That can't be right," Tom said, eyebrows furrowing.

"Well, there was something written down but it was often just a complaint like 'shortness of breath' or 'vomiting' and sometimes a finding like 'fever'. Pretty non-specific and not a diagnosis."

"Well, you know interns are more comfortable with discharge diagnoses."

"I've heard you say that before. Why is that?"

"It's a bit of a problem with our medical education system. Ever since Flexner, 100 years ago, the bulk of medical clinical experience comes in a hospital.

"And, before you can play with my head, I'll tell you why. It's because the patients are pretty much all in one place so there's not any wasted time travelling around. And, in that one place there's a variety of sickness so students can get a fair amount of experience concentrated in their time."

"Most educators are themselves committed to the hospital as their base and have become very comfortable with that as their classroom. And the students see the progression of a hospitalization going from a 'chief complaint' to a final, discharge diagnosis. They come to see the admitting diagnosis as a vague entity to be tested and refined during the hospital stay. So, naturally, recent graduates think the same way."

"But don't they know how the admitting diagnosis is used to predict length of stay and all that?"

"I bet they don't. I didn't either when I graduated. That's what we call 'administrivia'-not something real doctors care about."

"Well, they're wrong," said Beverly. "And you know it. So what are we going to do about it?"

"Well, I guess I could arrange for you to lecture them. I'm pretty certain that would do the trick."

"Come on, Tom. I'm serious. This is a real wedge that the administrators can use to control parts of our programs. We need to be out in front here."

"Bev, I know all that. And I've had my fun with trying to change these attitudes before," Tom said with a sarcastic cant. "Have I told you about my time with the VA-DoD Clinical Guidelines Group?"

"A little. I mean you mentioned some of the people you worked with from the VA who were national experts."

" They weren't the problem. We all agreed that we could do good work together-and we did. Mostly. At least, at first."

"What was the problem, then?"

"Everybody else. Whenever I tried talking about the usefulness of guidelines the discussion quickly turned into concerns about 'cookbook medicine'."

"I remember you told me that you used to say that Betty Crocker did pretty well with cookbooks."

"Yes, and that got some laughs, but not a lot of converts. It wasn't until we got them to really look at the guidelines that they understood the science behind them and mostly got on board."

"Then what's the problem with just doing that again? I mean why not just get the interns to start looking at the guidelines. I thought that was part of the reason for them-to be teaching tools."

"You're right, they were. But just like everything else in this profession, the guidelines got monetized and turned into some kind of administrative tool. Insurance companies began using the criteria as ways to limit admission-or payment-and to predict how long someone should stay in the hospital."

"Yes, but that information is helpful … "

"Bev, you're sounding like an administrator."

"I am an administrator, Tom. I'm not a doctor. So what's the … "

"Two things, at least. First is the fact that not every case of pneumonia is like every other case of pneumonia. The guidelines try to accommodate for that by making allowance for age and extent of disease but people are just different. Because the guideline use became monetized, they also became much more complex, trying to account for all kinds of variables that previously were handled by the physician rather automatically."

"But isn't the science still there?"

"Only if you believe that we are able to create a different 'cookbook' for every cook and every kitchen-and that is not what Betty Crocker did."

"What's the other thing?"

"You've been up on the wards. You know what our patients-and the bulk of hospitalized patients all over-are like. How many of them really fit into a single guideline?"

"What do you mean?"

"When your 69 year old woman with diabetes, frequent urinary tract infections and recently treated for breast cancer comes in with pneumonia and her diabetes is out of control and her immune system is knocked down, how well does a single guideline fit her situation?"

"Oh, I see … "

"Or how about the middle-aged man with multiple sclerosis who shows up on steroids with a urinary tract infection and pneumonia but doesn't meet criteria for either one because his temperature isn't high enough? What then?"

"OK, I got it. What do we do?"

"Well, the monetized system doesn't allow for that. It wants a firm and final diagnosis at admission to predict resource use and length of stay. The guideline has become a tool to control the cost of heath care. It is no longer a teaching tool. And I no longer champion the cause. The tools have been either allowed to become outdated or they are 'updated' with cost-containment as their purpose. And with our aging population, single guidelines become less and less applicable to the sick people who 'qualify' for hospital admission."

"What's the answer, then?"

"Damned if I know," Tom said, shaking his head and scratching the back of his neck. "But for now, I'll talk with Dick Abert and try to come up with a plan."

"Before you do that, I have some other information," Bev said smiling at him. "I also have two things you should know. One is that Nancy chose which guideline to apply when the admitting diagnosis was vague and she chose one that was not the same as the discharge diagnosis about a third of the time. So some of her primary data is suspect."

Tom whistled. And grinned.

Bev went on, "and the other thing is that about a third of the patients that did not meet criteria on admission did meet criteria the next day. Your interns are actually pretty keen about sensing who is sick-even if the guideline isn't."

"Great stuff! Where is that information?" Tom asked shuffling through the printouts.

"All in here," Beverly said as she handed Tom the thumb drive on which she had downloaded all the information.

CHAPTER 7

Monday September 16

en Nealy chose not to point out the nail changes on Mr. Kinney during rounds. He wanted to wait until he had some confirmation of his suspicion from the lab. He didn't even mention his new suspicion to Susan over lunch. He had told her about missing the boat on the lead toxicity but did not tell her of his new idea. They talked mostly about things they might do on an upcoming weekend. Omitting this point in their conversation made Ben a little uneasy; he and Susan had dated for several months and he had become accustomed to sharing even private thoughts with her. Leaving her out of his thoughts about another explanation for Kinney's symptoms also raised the specter of what she might say if he was right. Susan could be expected to want to know when this new idea occurred. Conversation for the rest of the lunch was restrained and somewhat oblique.

At the end of lunch, Susan had returned to the emergency area and Ben had gone to the library. Most of the trainees used PubMed to pull articles for education and Ben did a fair amount of that, as well. But he really liked the feel of holding a book in his hands and often went to the library for a specific reason. One of his valued professors in medical school could always be found right after lunch in the library sitting at the table where the most recent issue of all medical journals could be found. Ben had learned to emulate this practice at least a couple of times a week. He would read the main articles in major journals for an hour or so before going back to the ward.

When he did return to the ward, he sat down at the computer and sought out recent lab results on Mr. Kinney. Pleased and not completely surprised by the result when he got it he then sought out Dr. Hacker for discussion.

"Again with the coming to my office after rounds?" Hacker commented with raised eyebrows.

"I've got some new findings and I need guidance. I went and played like somebody else and started all over with Mr. Kinney."

"What's up?"

"I didn't bring this up on rounds today because Mrs. Kinney was in the room, but he's got Mee's lines on his nails and … "

"Whoa," Hacker interrupted. "I thought the lead level was zero."

"It was. So I tried arsenic. And it's definitely there."

"Arsenic! The other heavy metal."

"I did a little calculation on the growth rate of thumbnails and I think the date of the injury was about two months ago-and that's when his symptoms first began."

"And how do you think he got exposed?"

"He's a farmer and I first thought it might be tainted well water. But he has city water. I asked about how he handles crops and fertilizer and weed control and all that and he seems knowledgeable about what he doing and there's no hint of arsenicals."

"That *he* knows of."

"Exactly. And that's why I'm here. I think it's highly likely that she is poisoning him and I don't know what to do about it. I mean, I'm not Gregory House and I don't go rummaging around in other people's houses."

"No. That's not our job at all. But I do have some experience with a similar case over a year ago. And I have an idea about what we're going to do. Sit down and let's make a phone call."

CHAPTER 8

Thursday, September 19

Tom Bolling took his chicken salad and iced tea from the cafeteria line and joined the cardiology division in the doctors' dining room. They had agreed to a meeting to discuss their concerns about filling the vacancies in the division as a result of last year's events. Since one of the vacancies belonged to the former chief of division, Wilford Adamson, Tom had asked Mike Barone to take the chief's position with the concurrence of the academic partner.

Barone was a very capable clinician, a house staff perennial teaching favorite, and a careful clinical researcher but was a total unknown as an administrator. Tom genuinely liked Mike but definitely had some qualms about his ability to oversee the division. Cardiologists at New City were proud of their work and their status and generally each went their own way. Running the division was like herding frogs. Adamson had been effective in his own way, often by simply being the spokesperson for the majority opinion within the division. As far as Tom was aware, Wilford had never tried to persuade the division to change their position on any subject. Tom recognized that Wil was the kind of leader that said, "where are they going? I've got to get in front of them because I'm their leader."

But he had no idea what kind of leader Mike Barone was going to turn out to be. Since Wilford's death and the ultimate vacancy in the division chair, Tom had started dropping in to Mike's office at least once a week, often toward the end of the day. He would tell Mike something about the kind of administrative headache he, Tom, was facing at the time-and there was never a dearth of opportunities to talk about. Tom would muse out loud about the situation, provide information about the arguments on each side of the question and then 'announce' how he saw it and what he was going to do about it. And then he got up and left the office. For his part, Mike always sat there quietly and listened. Tom expected that Mike was soaking up insight into the myriad administrative tasks facing them and, he hoped, also picking up some background and reasoning for decisions that would have to be made.

Tom placed his salad and tea next to Mike's seat, nodded to others at the table and sat quietly eating while they discussed their own issues. When he had finished eating he indicated to Mike that he was ready for discussion and Mike called for everyone's attention.

"Tom, we thank you for taking time to sit down with us to discuss our thoughts and concerns about recruiting for these vacancies. We have some anxiety about how best to fill these slots and the impact the newcomers will make on our activities and income."

Tom remained seated and said, "I expect that you all know it was my initial intention to recruit someone from outside to fill Wilford's position. But now that I have come to the conclusion that Mike is the right guy for that position-and I see you have all agreed-I think I should make my position clear to you about recruiting."

"You may or may not know this," he went on, "but I have a job that requires a fair amount of my time and effort every day." There was some shuffling around as he said this and Tom knew there were those who thought his job was mostly ceremonial. "Recruiting within any division really is best done from within the division. Certainly better than if done by me." At this, there were some grins and an occasional tittering.

"I understand," Tom continued, "that there is some apprehension among you about income and I have some concerns about the workload volume that has decreased with these two vacancies. Our concerns in this regard are not dissimilar. But I prefer that the solution be yours and not mine. . . or the hospital director's." Several heads popped upright at this comment and it appeared that some were now paying more attention than before.

"So, I am here to tell you what I have told Mike. The role I will play in your recruiting will be supportive and consultative, not primary. As each of you know, most of you were recruited to come or to stay here by Wilford. He found you, offered you the job and made a place for you in the hospital and the division. Now that's Mike's job. It's a tough job, as you probably know. It will involve time spent on the phone trying to locate individuals with the right background, credentials and interest to be a positive addition to the division. Then he will have to convince those individuals to make a visit and all of you will be a part of deciding whether that person 'fits' here. At some point in the recruiting cycle, the newcomer will want something that you and Mike can't give them-new equipment, for instance. And that will be my job to try to meet those needs so you can get the person you want to join you."

One of the older cardiologists in the rear of the room raised his hand.

Tom waited until Mike recognized the questioner by saying, "Yes Pete?"

"Why don't we just run some ads in the journals and see who's interested?"

Mike looked at Tom who slowly said, "Good question, Pete. And my answer is this: 'Who reads ads about vacancies?' People who are looking to move, that's who. And I know people move for several different reasons. But I don't think we should limit ourselves to recruiting people who are ready to leave their current employment for whatever reason. I really want us to be attracting and hiring people who get comfortable with where they are. I expect to get the right ones we may have to work a little to get them to leave someplace that they have found comfortable."

As Tom had suspected most of the cardiologists were thinking that he would do all the work of recruiting and they would remain distant from the process until something went wrong and then they would be the most outspoken of critics. Tom had faced many circumstances in his career where he heard "If you had only asked me, I could have told you what was the better thing to do." He had now firmly positioned the responsibility for filling gaps in the Cardiology Division to the members of that division. They were assessing this reversal in the state of affairs and perhaps beginning to see the 'up' side as he took his plate and left the dining room.

CHAPTER 9

Thursday, September 19

Ben was in George Hacker's office sitting next to Hacker at his desk as they talked on the conference line to the Sheriff's office in the county up north. At George's direction they had consulted with the hospital legal staff after confirming that Mr. Kinney 's exposure to arsenic did not seem accidental. Counsel for New City, a middle-aged friend of Sam Mastone, was first and foremost concerned about the appearance of New City in any part of a legal case. His advice was to carefully divest the role of the hospital and its staff from the case as fully as possible.

Ben listened quietly while George repeatedly asked counsel how they were to accomplish that separation while they were the ones who had discovered the poisoning. Counsel was unsure of that and asked for some time to research it. He called George back a few hours later with a step-wise plan involving a call to the local prosecutor in the county up north. The New City counsel had provided the name and contact information for that prosecutor and George had immediately called her.

Their discussion with the prosecutor was an interesting diversion for Ben from the medical aspects of Mr. Kinney's case. The prosecutor was more than passingly interested and took as much time in obtaining a history of Mr. Kinney's medical affliction as any intern. Throughout her questioning, she kept asking Ben, "How do you know that?" about specific facts such as the timing of probable first dosing with arsenic, attribution of Mr. Kinney's medical symptoms to arsenic exposure and validity of the urine sample test.

At the conclusion of their conversation she indicated she would be pursuing a warrant to search the farm for evidence. Ben immediately felt anxiety and said, "What if I'm wrong about this?"

"Do you think it is possible that you are wrong?" the prosecutor had asked.

Ben tried to explain that he knew he was right about the connection between arsenic and Mr. Kinney's symptoms but he was unsure of the role played by the wife.

George and the prosecutor both had assured Ben that the right thing to do was to investigate and then draw conclusions. If the poisoning was inadvertent the investigation could be explained as a public health issue. Ben felt only slightly better at that point. The prosecutor's office took the medical information and obtained a warrant for the Kinney farmhouse and investigators were now on the line to discuss their initial findings. Ben wasn't sure why the prosecutor had allowed him and Hacker to listen in on this call from the field investigator but he was excited to be there. But he was also a little bit apprehensive.

Ben had never been involved in anything like this before and was nervous. He had started this ball rolling and realized he was setting Mrs. Kinney up for attempted murder charges but because he was unsure how things would unfold his anxiety was evident.

"Hacker put the phone on mute and said, "Hey, this is the right thing to do. You know it, right?"

"Yeah, I do. But it's a big unknown."

"We will deal with the reality. OK?"

"Yes. I agree," Ben agreed, feeling a little better about the risk.

Hatcher released the mute button and they waited.

"Sgt., are you ready to discuss?" asked the prosecutor and few minutes later.

"Are we ever," came the answer.

"Tell me your tale," said the prosecutor again, "Just like you'll tell it to the jury."

"Since we were looking for something specific and since our warrant included outbuildings, we started with the barn out back."

"First," interrupted the prosecutor. "Were there any family members present?'

"No m'am. We understood that the kids live elsewhere and the wife was at the hospital."

"That's right," Hacker interjected. "We were trying to keep her out of the way."

"Well," drawled the investigator, "she wasn't here and we went to the barn. Found several types of weed control and insecticide sprays but none with arsenic."

Ben's heart sunk. Could he have been wrong?

"But then we went in the house-doors all unlocked, by the way- and looked in the kitchen," the investigator continued. "And we hit the jackpot!"

Ben almost jumped out of the chair. He and Hacker both leaned forward as if they could get the information from the conference call more quickly.

"Yep." The investigator was obviously enjoying slow walking his information. "In the back of the pantry we found a brown glass jar with a homemade label saying it contained 'Ginger'. The label underneath says 'arsenic trioxide'. White powder, kinda granular, no odor."

"Did you get the bottle to bring to the lab?" asked the prosecutor.

Taking no umbrage at the possible suggestion that he didn't know how to do his job the investigator drawled, "Oh yes, m'am. We got the bottle and so much more."

"What?" spoke several voices on the line almost simultaneously.

"Well, since it looked so much like sugar I thought we'd just check the sugar bowl. Sitting right there on the kitchen table. Looks to me like about a 50-50 mix.

"Did you get … "

"Yes, m'am. We got the sugar bowl and we handled it with gloves so any fingerprints are still there. I think we're through here."

"I think so, too, Sgt. Thank you for a job well done."

"Yes, M'am. We'll be back in about thirty minutes." He disconnected.

The prosecutor spoke next, "Thank you, doctors. I think we have a pretty solid case here with your information and these findings. I appreciate your bringing this to my attention." And she disconnected, leaving only Hacker and Ben and the New City legal counsel on the line.

"I'm off," said counsel as he hung up. The remaining pair turned to each other and smacked a high five.

CHAPTER 10

Friday, September 27

Tom Bolling walked into the lobby from the parking garage and immediately caught the eye of Nick the barista. They each made head movements indicating that a message sent had been received. A few other customers were clustered in line to order but there were no others at the cash register so Tom proceeded there and paid. The clerk was punching a hole in his reward card when Nick handed him his drink.

"Here you go, sir."

"Thanks Nick. You know, sometimes your Black Eye may be the only reason I get through the day."

"I'll be here all week, doc."

"I know. You tell me that every week. You're the Lenny Bruce of Green Bean."

"I should be so good."

Tom took his cup and entered the executive suite and turned to his office area.

Mary Brighthouse looked up and said, "Mr. Mastone is really fired up this morning. He got a call from someone downtown."

"Any idea about the subject?"

"No, but I'm sure it'll come up at the morning meeting."

"Great way to start. Got any aspirin?"

"No, but Beverly has some Advil."

Tom got some Advil from Beverly, who always had a small container in her pocket. However, she no idea about what was upsetting Sam and couldn't help there.

"Let's just get in there and face the music and get on with the day," Tom mumbled on his way to the Conference Room.

Sam Mastone was already seated at the head of the table when Tom and Beverly entered. Since he usually waited in his office and entered virtually on the stroke of eight o'clock, his presence prior to that was one indication that he had issues to discuss at the meeting. Another indication was his clenched left hand.

"Sam," Tom said in greeting. He received a nod of recognition just as Roslyn Burke and Alena Preston joined them at the table.

Sam started abruptly by saying, "I received a call this morning from the editor of the sports section in the paper. He and his daughter were in the emergency area last evening and were treated rudely by the clerk. I want to know what happened."

Tom blurted the obvious, "Didn't the editor tell you what happened?"

"Not exactly. He said they were treated rudely. That's all. But he said it seven times and very loudly." He turned to Roslyn, "What happened down there? That clerk works for you doesn't she?"

Slightly flustered at this Roslyn managed to get out, "Yes, the clerks are part of Nursing, but . . ."

"Well you get that girl up here right now and find out what happened?"

Roslyn stared at Sam.

"What's the matter?" he asked, in a voice that was still too loud.

"First, that tour ended at seven this morning and all personnel have left the hospital by now," she said gaining control of her feelings. "And, second, the clerk in the emergency area at night is not a 'girl'. It's one of our male clerks, his name is Allen."

"Well, I want you to call him and find out what happened down there. I want an explanation why I have to hear about rude behavior from clerical staff before coffee in the morning."

Roslyn and Alena got up from the table and left the conference room. Sam took a deep breath and turned to Tom. "We have these surveys that say our patients think we are wonderful. How can we have such good survey reports and I still get these kinds of calls?"

"Well, Sam, there's a lot to be said on patient satisfaction surveys starting with the fact that there's really only two kinds. There's one to make you, the hospital director feel good and one that you can actually use to improve patient service. Perhaps you've got the wrong one."

"What do you mean? We're paying good money for that survey, twice a year even."

"Difference isn't in the cost, it's in the value."

"You're talking that 'quality and performance' lingo again, aren't you?"

"That's right. But the words do mean something. What is the survey you're using?"

"Big name. Can't remember it right now but its well known at the ACHE." Sam may have thought that mentioning an endorsement from the American College of Healthcare Executives would impress Tom, but he was mistaken.

"OK. I know the survey you mean. Questions about 'could you understand your doctor or nurse'? and 'did you understand what was going to happen after discharge'?, right?"

"Well, it's been a while since I looked at the actual questions but yeah, I think that's about right." Sam was becoming more calm.

"Probably some questions about the food and the cleanliness of the hospital, too?"

"Of course. I think all the important areas are touched on."

"How do you survey patients?"

"Very clean operation, Tom" Sam felt he was on familiar ground. "Every six months we hand out a survey to every patient in the hospital and ask them to complete it before discharge. Nurses collect them on the wards and turn them in to Andy and the IT guys feed them into a scanner and give me the results." Sam leaned back proudly.

"Well, I see several areas where you are not going to get the best results from that kind of survey." Tom said firmly as he sipped his coffee.

"What do you mean?" Sam said sitting forward suddenly.

"That's a 'feel good' survey. Everybody knows that. The nurses probably 'help' some of the patients to fill out the forms and even if there is a problem identified you don't know what it means, usually."

"Yes, we do."

"What was the last time you learned something from that survey and made a change?"

"I don't remember but. . . "

"You're asking the wrong questions, that's all. You aren't asking what patients really care about."

"How do you know?"

"Sam, I ran a major hospital in the Air Force, remember. We scuttled that survey you're using and built one the old fashioned way. We asked patients what made their hospital stay good, better or best." Tom paused at this and waited until Sam was about to speak before going on. "And then we asked them what that looked like."

Sam indicated with his hands that Tom should continue the story.

"We found out, for instance, that patients think clerks are rude if they don't know why the patient is there or if they don't make eye contact when talking to them."

"Really?'

"Yeah. I'll bet you a cup of coffee that Allen is accused of being rude because he was not making eye contact with the editor. That's all. And our survey told us when that was happening and exactly what to do about it. Train the clerks to make eye contact."

"Maybe we could do that here, then." Sam almost seemed calm as he said this.

"Well, there's a company that markets a patient oriented survey. I'll get their information for you. They do a mailing to recently discharged patients and they get 75-80 percent response!"

"Really? I think most cold call surveys get about 20 percent."

"That's right. But this isn't really a cold call. These patients would like to tell you what you did well and what didn't go right."

"Apparently we could use that,"

"Here's a fun fact: this survey does not ask about the food or the cleanliness."

"What? Those are very important aspects of quality care."

"Well, they are not 'satisfiers', Sam. Patients will tell you they didn't come to the hospital for the food; if it's bad it is a real dissatisfier but you can't make the food good enough to make the care they get seem wonderful. Same thing about the cleanliness. Your hospital better be clean or it becomes a dissatisfier. But shiny floors and glistening brass will not make up for sloppy care."

"I don't get the 'satisfier'-'dissatisfier' disconnect." Sam looked puzzled at this seeming paradox.

"Well." Tom said with a little smile, "all I can tell you is they are not opposite ends of the same spectrum."

"What? How can that be if . . ." Sam was interrupted by the return of the nurse executives. He paused while Roslyn and Alena returned to their seats. Then, recovering a little of his former anger, he asked, "Did you talk to this Allen?"

"Yes, I did," Roslyn said a little stiffly. "He remembers the man, who was quite demanding, by the way. Allen said he was not rude, called the man 'sir' and all that but he was busy pulling up charts and checking people out and the guy hollered at him twice about not looking at him when he talked to him."

There was a long pause. Roslyn felt her employee had been unfairly represented and she stared at the director. Sam nodded to her, then turned to Tom and asked, "What are you drinking?"

CHAPTER 11

Wednesday, October 2

Richard Abert, Chairman of Medicine at New City was sitting in front of Tom Bolling's desk. A tall thin man with graying hair, his posture indicated discomfort as Tom spoke, "Come on, Dick. This is something we need to do. And I really want your help in getting it done."

"I just don't see it, Tom. You know we have an attending down there in the intern clinic but they don't run everything by her and she has her own patients during that time."

"I know Janey is down there and that's why I think she could be the first line of defense for us to help these young guys and gals learn about this part of the 'arc of medical care'.

"It's not an arc, it's an intrusion. We spend all day and night trying to get these kids to get the dose of drugs right. We don't have time to teach them your administrative tricks, too."

"Hold on, Dick. These are not 'my' requirements. I trust you do understand that the insurance funding for care on your service was short some $40,000 since the first of July?

"I know you said that but I don't have that kind of information at my fingertips." Abert was pushing a point he had made repeatedly since Tom arrived as chief of staff: that he and the other Chairmen did not have access to many of the databases that Tom and Sam brought up at various times and used to push the clinical chairs toward more involvement in the financial part of medicine. Tom actually sympathized with the chairs and had argued several times with Sam about getting the Chairs involved in primary data analysis; so far his arguments were stymied by Sam's insistence that there weren't resources enough for the task.

Now that lack of information was creating a barrier for Tom dealing with the chief of medicine. New City's program of having a follow-up clinic for interns had been one of the earliest in the country. For years the program had been a major reason many trainees wanted to do their internship at New City. Each intern was assigned a 'panel' of patients and could add patients to that panel when they were discharged from an inpatient stay. The clinics were held in the afternoons and each intern controlled their own appointments. They also ordered the laboratory or imaging tests they felt necessary to care for their individual patients and, when necessary, they could admit patients to the hospital for further care. The issue of 'inappropriate' admissions coming from these clinics suggested that the interns were insufficiently trained in recognizing who needed inpatient care. Dick Abert knew that argument was likely true but felt the data in that regard should be his to evaluate and not Sam Mastone's.

Tom lowered his chin and stared at Dick. "I'm not expecting you to have the data at your fingertips and play 'first responder'," he said. "I am asking that you get involved now that you do have the data in your hands. Beverly and I have checked the data three different ways and we have a problem and its caused by the interns on your service and it has got to stop." Tom was getting a little warm under the collar. He could identify with the desire of the chairs to not get blindsided by these accusations of seeming malfeasance. He had experience with that in the Air Force when he was the one getting blindsided. But he still felt he was not playing unfairly with them and he really needed their assistance in making necessary changes.

"Look, Tom, I'm not accusing you of having switched to the dark side, even if you are a surgeon. I'm just saying that when I hear about these issues, it's gone on for months and some magical dollar figure is quoted and I feel like my head is on the block. Meantime the Chair at the school wants more face time spent on clinical teaching and I don't have any answers." He was repeating a recurring theme of the tension always present in a for-profit hospital where medical interns and residents are learning. The very process of education adds time and cost to the process of medical care and when cost-reduction issues occurred, the educational program always floated to the top of the discussion.

Tom knew the men and women who held the chairs in New City and none of them were profligate with the resources they were given to support their educational program. They were responsible individuals and, like most physicians, felt that they had the capacity to solve virtually any problem. Tom remembered what one of his former commanders told him as he left the military. "Tom," the general had said, " those of us at command are very proud of you. We know you are a capable administrator and we believe if the people at New City give you enough time you can solve any problem they have." Then the general smiled and said, "And we know they'll never give you enough time."

And, of course, that was prophecy fulfilled. Tom realized that sometime he was passing that lack of time down to the chairs and he wanted to be able to do differently. The particular issue in this case was not actually time but information, his own inability to get Mastone to support such information to the chairs was the real issue. Mastone could not see the value of having the chairs responsible for the data and solving problems before they grew to the $40,000 level because Sam thought such problem-solving was his responsibility. Tom realized he would have to make a better and more effective argument about data sharing in the very near future.

"All right. I say to you again, I've tried over and over to get you and the chairs in the loop on some of the administrative databases so you can watch for issues and catch them when they develop. But Sam keeps dragging his feet. I promise I'll stay on that but right now we need to do something about these inappropriate admissions!"

Abert looked steadily at Tom for a few moments. The two of them had already talked about the definition of 'inappropriate' and had finally agreed to set aside their own feelings about the measuring device. Tom knew that Abert was being put in a difficult position with his Chairman at the University and had tried to provide him some defense for a discussion with the Chairman later.

The University was heavily dependent upon the training hospitals to provide the stipend for trainees; every chairman knew that but often acted as if the University was doing the hospital a giant favor by assigning trainees there. Tom intended the information about the financial shortfall that could be directly attributed to the presence of the trainees to be a sharp arrow in Abert's quiver in dealing with the University. However, it was not clear that Dick had seen the value of that information yet.

Abert took a breath and with a slight nod said, "I'll ask M.E. to talk with the interns about this but you need to give her all the information and you should be there to add some gravitas."

"You mean you're not going to be there." Tom made this a statement but the implied question hung in the air for half a minute before Abert answered as he pulled himself to full height while sitting.

"Right. At this time I need to maintain my distance from activities that appear to be at odds with our educational program."

"Oh for God's sake, Dick. Don't go all Holier-than-Thou on me. We've both been through medical school and residency training and we both know there's a giant gap in that education about what's needed to succeed in the real world of the practice of medicine. And one of the biggest gaps involves not understanding where the money comes from. What about getting Janey more involved in decisions to admit?"

"Janey has her own panel and is quite busy seeing those patients during her time in the clinic. If the interns start queuing up to ask her every little question both systems will bog down."

"Dick, you know I'm not suggesting that they check every decision with her, just whether they should admit someone," Tom said soothingly. He knew that Dick was trying to be of assistance in solving the problem while maintaining a position aloof from the income stream. And Tom wanted Dick's help. "Can we agree on that little change?"

"Well, you and M.E. can help these poorly educated PG-1s get up to speed on that important issue. I hope it works." Tom thought on what was being said. He knew Mary Elizabeth Palmieri, the chief resident in Internal Medicine. She was well known around the hospital as the most likely to remain calm in the middle of a crisis that most had ever seen. And she was a very smart physician, too. M.E., as she was known, was possibly better suited to a presentation like this to young house officers than any of the faculty. Tom realized Dick Abert was not completely undercutting his effort; he was actually giving Tom a capable arrow in his own quiver. He smiled and nodded in agreement and Dick got up to leave.

As the Chairman of Medicine left his office, Tom leaned back in his chair and thought, wryly, "Well that went well, didn't it?"

CHAPTER 12

Thursday, October 24

Tom Bolling sat in his usual prominent seat in the front row of the auditorium as Ben Nealy and George Hacker presented the case of Mr. Kinney at weekly Grand Rounds: a mysterious case of weight loss without anatomic findings. Academic Grand Rounds was a staple of university training programs in internal medicine. The structure allowed for the in-depth clinical presentation of a patient case to an audience of seasoned clinicians and trainees of all stripes. The format followed the case presentation with discussion of the physiology behind signs and symptoms, diagnostic tests and current treatment of the condition. Presenters often spent as much time in preparation as they normally did on a publication for national journals. For that reason, Grand Rounds usually allowed one of the faculty members to make the in-depth presentation; involvement of a trainee was commonly limited to presentation of the case. Physicians who regularly attended Grand Rounds were awarded an hour of credit toward their medical licensing requirement for Continuing Medical Education each year.

Ben Nealy, however, was part of the scientific exposition as well as making the case presentation at the outset. His part involved discussion of the normal growth and development of fingernails and the pathology of characteristic lines across the nails in cases of heavy metal poisoning. These lines, known as Mee's lines, were named for the Dutch physician who described them in 1919. Ben's presentation focused on normal nail formation and growth and how distance of the Mee's lines from the nail bed could be used to time the intake of poison.

The case had been a major topic of conversation for a couple of weeks throughout the hospital when the diagnosis was made and that discussion became more interesting when Mrs. Kinney was arrested for attempted murder. The focus of the Grand Rounds by Nealy and Hacker, however, was more on the pathology of heavy metal poisoning and the various ways it could occur environmentally with particular attention to arsenic.

The two presenters had carefully marked off the circumstance in the case of how the particular heavy metal, in this instance, arsenic, was introduced but their emphasis in discussion was how the interruption of intake led to the Mee's lines and other signs and symptoms. Their presentation on heavy metal poisoning emphasized the need for suspicion early in the course and careful re-examination of the patient at intervals to find the changes in the fingernails.

Tom was quite pleased with their presentation and glad that there had not been some general news flash implicating New City. Coverage in the newspapers had been fair and mentioned the hospital only as the place of diagnosis.

As Hacker finished the presentation and room lights came up, he asked for questions. The audience applauded politely and many members rose from their seats to leave the auditorium. Some of those in attendance knew slightly more of the story but were not interested in using this setting to pursue it.

One, however, was. A young woman stood and asked, "Dr. Hacker, how often do you think something like this happens?"

He replied, carefully misinterpreting her question, "I believe we gave figures on the occurrence of heavy metal poisoning in the United States since 1950."

"I mean, how often does someone try to kill somebody with arsenic? That seems a little old-fashioned, doesn't it?"

"We purposefully chose not to make this Grand Rounds about the attempted murder but to focus on the clinical signs and metabolic disturbances from heavy metals," he said looking around the room for another questioner.

"But what made you so sure it was his wife in this case?" the young woman persisted.

Beverly leaned toward Tom and whispered. He stood and said, "Thank you, Drs. Nealy and Hacker for this in-depth presentation about heavy metal toxicity." And he then led another, shorter round of applause. While he was holding everyone's attention near the front of the auditorium, Beverly approached the young woman and said, "This is a medical teaching conference and not the place for your investigative reporting. I'll walk with you to the door." Without much ado the questioner was herded out of the room. At the exit to the outside Beverly spoke firmly to the young woman, "There is no place for you to be questioning our physicians about their work. If you have questions about the legal proceedings, talk to the police or to the lawyers in the case. Understood?" She received a brief nod of understanding and watched the reporter leave the hospital grounds.

As Ben left the stage Tom met him at the foot of the stairs. "That was a very good pick-up, Ben. It makes me proud when the 'fleas' do something this impressive!"

Before Ben respond, he realized that Tom was actually complimenting him while aiming a little barb at George Hacker standing behind him.

Hacker said, "And we didn't even have to wait for the dog to die."

Tom grinned and shook both of their hands. "Really good, guys. Did you ever hear anything about why the wife was trying to kill him?"

Hacker responded, "Yes, we did. Not for publication, of course, but the prosecutor talked to me a week or so ago about getting reports on the actual arsenic levels in the blood and urine. She said the wife crumped when confronted and admitted it all. She said Kinney had 'run around on her' twenty some odd years ago and she had never forgiven him."

"Woman scorned," Tom chuckled and all three nodded.

"Really good. Save a life and make an excellent teaching program. We should have more of that." Tom reiterated as he patted both men on their back.

CHAPTER 13

Saturday, November 2

Ron Looney was sitting at his breakfast table. Another Saturday morning and Homicide Detective Looney was next up for any homicide in the city. Ron and his partner Gene Novalchek had each hoped for different reasons that their rotation would have ended on Friday. But the uniquely quiet night in Cincinnati brought them unscathed into Saturday. Ron was about to finish his breakfast-specifically, he was starting on the last pancake when his cell phone rang. He looked at the caller ID and grimaced at his wife, Meg across the table. "It's not even eight o'clock and I've still got a pancake and two slices of bacon to go."

"Wrap the bacon in the pancake and tell Gene you had a burrito," Meg said without smiling.

"A detective gets no respect in his own household," Ron said as he answered the call.

"Walker." Ron used his 'inside the department' nickname.

As he listened he did what Meg suggested and rolled up the bacon strips in the pancake and grinned at her. She blew him a kiss and went to fill his travel coffee cup.

"Sounds bad," he said, hanging up. "But likely no rush. All the dying's already been done. No reason I'll be late tonight."

He shrugged into his jacket, kissed Meg, grabbed the bacon burrito in one hand and his coffee cup in the other and headed for the door. Ron Looney-known to his associates as 'Walker' for his tendency to foot patrol when assigned to neighborhoods-was on his way to what he hoped was the first and last of his callouts for the day.

Ron had retired from the Air Force as a Senior Master Sergeant in the Security Police with many years experience as a criminal investigator and a degree in Criminal Justice. Meg's brother, Paul Andicott, a long-time member of Cincinnati's finest in the Robbery Division got Ron an interview with the department after retirement. Now, fourteen years later, Ron was a valued detective and member of the Homicide Division. Ron was a 'good ole boy' from farmland Arkansas who joined the military right out of high school and who had progressed on hard work, a cool head under fire and solid instincts about people.

Perhaps the most notable thing about Ron was his lack of interest in climbing the hierarchical ladder in the department. On two occasions his captain, Arne Thorason had pushed him to take the lieutenant's test. Ron just delayed the first time and missed the application deadline. The second time he was pulled into Thorason's office to discuss the matter. He explained his attitude toward such a job. He had been raised on a farm in southeast Arkansas and had chores to do every day from the time he could walk. His formal school experience did not allow after school activities because his chores were important to the family and the farm. He had explained to Captain Thorason that he thought a man should abide by what his father told him about how to approach a job.

"If you work for the man," his father said with his usual sagacity and minimum of words, "then work for the man."

In the Air Force when he had earned his degree and first been promoted to Technical Sergeant the office he led became less functional. Ron had been uneasy about telling others how, or when, to do their job and relied completely on the morality of each man to do his job right. Slackers he put on useless tasks to keep them out of the way. And he was personally unhappy not doing the fieldwork of investigations. After a very short period he was technically demoted back to the field, without losing a stripe, and sent to Criminal Investigative School. The Air Force kept him in the field at his request from then on. And that was what he wanted Captain Thorason to do for him.

As he drove to the neighborhood where had had been directed, Ron spent little time thinking about the details he had been given on the case. His experience was that the third hand report often contained either gross exaggerations or subtle misleadings. He preferred to spend the time at the scene to get his own perspective on events and people involved. But he did make sure that he finished the bacon burrito before he parked and started toward the scene. The department frowned on eating on the job; besides, Gene would have wanted to talk about it.

As Ron crossed the street from where he had parked he saw Gene approaching from down the block. Gene Novalchek inherited more characteristics from his Swedish mother than his Polish father. At six feet tall and 190 pounds he looked more like a professional golfer than the cruiserweight boxer which he was. His face, lean and long did not often hide his feelings and when his bushy eyebrows came together acquaintances knew a storm was brewing. This did not often happen, though, because Gene was generally and smiling and happy man and so a bit of an oddity on the Homicide squad. Ron really enjoyed working with Gene for that reason. Just because other people spent their life killing others did not mean Ron and Gene had to wear a hard pucker all the time.

Ron had a high regard for the detectives in Homicide; they were diligent, hard-working individuals who clearly felt an obligation to not let perpetrators get away with murder. But, in spite of that high regard, Ron knew he would not have enjoyed his job if paired with almost anyone other than Gene. Ron's attitude of 'work for the man' had often made him somewhat at odds with other detectives who seemed ready to break early for lunch or to allow a single interview to be sufficient at times when Ron clearly thought otherwise. It wasn't something reflected in the outcomes in the Division since the closure rate for all teams was high. But Gene's partnership style was unobtrusive and allowed Ron to feel more like he was working the case with his approach and tactics, not on his own but with understanding support. They often talked through issues and the interpretation of clues as of one mind, although Gene's observations frequently added depth to the understanding of the case.

Gene waved at his partner and they started up the walk together toward the uniformed officer standing at the porch steps.

"Did you get to finish breakfast?" asked Gene.

"I ate it in the car," said Ron staring straight ahead and knowing what was coming.

"Well, I didn't even get to start. I put extra sugar in my coffee but I'm gonna have to go get some food pretty soon." One consistent aspect of Gene's daily interest was when would the team take time to eat. Lulls in conversation or during times of waiting for something to happen always ended up with Gene talking about food. Plus, he was so descriptive when he did talk about food, it became an interest of Ron's until he got hungry, also.

"Gene, we'll go when we can. Don't make that our goal for the day, OK?"

Gene turned to the uniformed officer and asked, "So what have you got?"

The young officer said, "Dead woman inside is Hannah Grant. Looks like a self-inflicted wound from a shotgun. Really messy. Husband was out here when it happened, talking to the neighbor. Neighbor is the guy in the sweats on the porch next door."

Ron asked, "And the husband is inside?"

"Yes," said the patrolman. "My partner's with him. He's pretty messed up, too. I've already called the M.E.."

"OK. Just keep the husband away and quiet. We'll be right in after we talk to the witness."

CHAPTER 14

Saturday, November 2

The neighbor, Alan Bronsky, was clearly agitated and talkative. According to him everything was usual until he went out to get his newspaper. Just then, Steven Grant came out his door and started a conversation.

"Are you saying that was unusual?" Gene asked.

"What? No. I meant there wasn't anything going on until then. That's all."

"What did you talk about?" Ron inquired as he looked around and noticed the thick hedge between the two yards.

"I dunno, just stuff, I guess. Little baseball, you know. He said he was going for a run."

"And he seemed normal and all?"

"Yeah, I guess. Him in sweats going for a run and me in a sweat suit going for breakfast. Pretty normal around here."

"That's all?"

"Well, yeah. Until he told me about her being upset and all that."

"What's that? What did he say about her?" Ron became more interested in the discussion.

"He said she was upset."

"Did he say why she was upset?"

"Kinda. I mean, yeah. He said they had a fight over something last night."

"Last night? Not this morning?"

"No, he said it was last night and he had to sleep on the sofa."

"Did he say what the fight was about?"

"I don't think so. He said it was stupid."

"Then what happened?' Ron probed.

"He said he decided he should go apologize and he ran back in the house. I was going to go in, too. But that's when I heard him yell and heard the gun go off."

"Tell me about that," said Ron.

"Steve had just opened the door and I heard him yelling 'No!' and like that. And then the gun went off and he came out the door and hollered 'She shot herself! Call 9-1-1'. And I ran in the house and called you guys."

"Wait a minute," said Gene. Did you see him go in the house? I mean before the gunshot?"

"Well, I don't think so. I mean I was looking at the newspaper. I think he just got to the door and got it open-but I really can't say for sure. When he yelled I looked up and saw him run in at the same time the gun went off."

"As far as you know, did the Grants have trouble in their marriage?"

"Not that I knew. He never talked about it."

"But this time he brought it up."

"Yeah. But he also said it was probably his fault and he had decided to go apologize when she shot herself."

'How do you know she shot herself?" Asked Gene, taking careful notes.

"Well, it couldn't be anyone else could it? I mean, Steve was out here and there's no one else in the house … "

"I see. Well, thank you sir. Please stay available, as we may want to talk to you again.

"Yeah, sure. OK"

The two detectives excused themselves and walked back to the crime scene house. They looked at each other sideways and Ron made a wry little smile as they approached the steps onto the porch.

Inside, they paused and took in the scene. The doorway from the porch entered into the near end of a living room space that ran the length of the front of the house. At the far end were two corner cabinets and in the center of the room were two sofas facing each other with a glass topped coffee table in between. A middle-aged man was sitting on the far couch with a blanket draped over his shoulders, his head in his hands, a uniformed policeman standing behind him. The end of the room near the outside door opened into a hallway with a stairway to the second floor. On the back wall a large archway led into a dining room that held an ornate glass-topped Queen Anne dining table with seating for six. One of the chairs had been spun around facing toward the living room. In the chair was what, at first glance, appeared to be a headless body draped in white.

The man on the couch did not recognize their presence. Gene and Ron nodded to the officer and slowly walked to the archway and stood close to the body. The body in the chair was a woman whose face and top of her head had been removed by a shotgun blast. The residue of the blast was on the ceiling toward the center of the room and some of the gore had dripped onto the tabletop. Truly, as the patrolman had said, messy. Both men took note of the minimal amount of blood around the chair.

Ron slowly circled the body, noticing that the woman was wearing a nightgown. A thought flickered through his head about identifying the body without a face and realized they would also not have dental records to help. As he stood behind her he noticed how the left shoulder strap had slid down her arm. She was very pale and the remaining hair on the back of her head hung down over the chair back. Ron noted the tinge of purplish color on her shoulder. He stooped down at the rear of the chair and looked under the chair for a moment and then stood up and took a deep breath. He and Gene made eye contact again and now they both made a wry grin.

The shotgun was lying beside the chair. Gene leaned over and sniffed at the barrel. He looked up and nodded. The gun had recently been fired. There did not appear to be anything else to see so the detectives moved into the living room to talk with the husband.

"Mr. Grant. I'm Detective Ron Looney and this is my partner, Gene Novalchek. We would like to talk to you about what happened."

No movement from the man on the couch. "Yeah, OK," came muffled through the blanket.

"Could you tell us just what happened here this morning, sir?"

Head up, he said, "She shot herself. Right in front of me."

"What happened before that?"

"This was all my fault. We argued last night and went to bed mad. Never supposed to do that."

"What did you argue about?" Gene asked quietly.

"Something stupid. Never should have happened. It's all my fault."

"What was the fight about, Mr. Grant?"

" I wanted us to go out to dinner and she wanted to cook something here."

"Really? That's what you argued about?"

"That's what started it. But then it spread to other things. Money. How I treat her. Things like that."

"And what happened then?" Gene nudged.

"She stormed upstairs and said I should sleep on the couch. She even threw my pillow and a blanket down."

"And then …?" Gene prodded.

"Then I slept down here … and got up with a crick in my neck and ate some cereal before she came down."

"What time was that?" asked Ron.

"I don't know, maybe about seven or so."

"And what happened then?"

"Well, she was still surly and not talking to me and I just stormed out to go run or something. If I had only stayed she would never have done anything like this." His head fell into the blanket again.

The detectives looked at each other and then Ron said, "Tell me about coming back in the house."

Steven was still and quiet for a moment and then took a deep breath and said, "When I opened the door she was sitting there with the gun, staring at me. like she was waiting for me to come in … and then … then she pulled the trigger … "

"Did you try to stop her?"

"What? I yelled, 'No' or 'Stop' or something and ran toward her but she didn't … stop … "

"And what did you do then?" asked Ron.

"I yelled at Bronsky to call 9-1-1 and came back to her. I guess I just sat here with her until that policeman made me leave."

"Anything else, Mr. Grant?' asked Gene.

"No, I don't think so. It's all a blur. This is all my fault."

CHAPTER 15

Saturday, November 2

Ben finished his ward work and drifted down to the Emergency Area to see if Susan would take a break and go get some coffee with him. The ED was a little on the quiet side at the moment, only four people in the various rooms and all were being taken care of while waiting for laboratory results or a call to imaging. Ben smiled at the receptionist, Jenny something, who was sitting at Carla's desk before going down to the nurses' station.

Susan Chang was chatting with another nurse and they both smiled as Ben walked up. Susan did not look at all Asian, in spite of the name. Her mother, single with an infant girl had married Albert Chang and taken his name for them both. Susan was strawberry blond with light skin and facial freckles over a small nose and fine cheekbones. Only 5 foot 6 inches in height she always seemed taller because of her way of wearing her hair. This day she was wearing a ponytail that came from the top of her head. She grinned at Ben and asked, "Finished upstairs?"

"Oh yeah. You know the work up there-it expands into the time given to it. I took control and shortened the time. Wanna get coffee?"

The other nurse said, quasi-innocently, "You know, we have a coffee pot right back here."

"But no place to sit and talk," Ben countered.

"Or to hold hands," she rejoined as Susan, to her credit, blushed. She and Ben had been dating for several months but the ED nurses kept treating their relationship like it was brand new.

"Oh come on," she said and pulled Ben toward the door to the hallway.

*   *   *

Twenty minutes later, as they re-entered the Emergency area, they noticed a clamor of activity in the main hallway around a new admission. Susan immediately inserted herself into the nursing activity and Ben watched from the hallway.

Police had brought in a vagrant from the downtown area where several homeless had started camping out. Residents at the VA and New City were aware the police would periodically clear the area even though there were no businesses nearby. Ben could hear the story from the sergeant who brought in the vagrant. He was explaining to the emergency resident that the guy smelled strongly of alcohol and was nearly comatose when they found him but he would rouse. They noticed that he had recently vomited on himself and they were concerned he might have aspirated. It was clear that the officers wanted to be rid of the issue; they were backing toward the door all the while they were commenting on the man's condition and their concerns.

The emergency resident was somewhat unsure of himself but was issuing some orders to the nurses when Ben moved over next to him and said quietly, "Let them get him cleaned up and then let's see what we got." The resident was a PGY1 and he looked relieved that Ben was there. The two of them stepped away and the nurses moved the man from the hallway gurney into one of the examining rooms. They carefully removed his worn and dirty clothes and washed his face of grime and vomit and quickly started an intravenous line before indicating that the physicians were welcome to begin their examination.

Ben had enjoyed his own rotation through emergency and so he followed the resident into the room to assess the man's condition. He was thin and had no discernable body fat. Clearly he was drunk and hardly able to interact with his environment.

"Hey, buddy," the resident called directly into the man's face. "What's your name?" There was not a sensible response. "Can you tell me your name?" he persisted. Again, he received no response.

Ben began looking around for the man's possessions and found a worn, ragtag backpack under the stinking clothes.

"Cop said he had held onto the bag like it was full of gold," one of the nurses explained.

Ben looked in the bag and found nothing that would help identify the man. The bag held an incredibly dirty handkerchief of plain linen, a Cincinnati Bearcat stocking cap that the old guy had been wearing, a worn-out toothbrush and a bottle of whisky that was nearly empty and a very dirty tie-dyed T-shirt.

Ben held up the cap and said, "A fan."

The resident said, "Bearcat. Hey, Bearcat. What's your name?"

The nurses were taking the man's temperature and blood pressure and the resident was trying to listen to his lungs and someone said, loudly, "Maybe that's his name-Bear Cat" and someone else said, "Or, Bear-y." And the man said, "Whaa?" And, of course, from then on he was known as "Barry".

'Barry' was incredibly drunk. The nurses had managed to find a vein and drew some blood and started an intravenous drip with glucose. They checked a blood sugar with a finger stick; it was 67 so they increased his intravenous fluid.

His temperature was 95 Fahrenheit on admission so the nurses covered him with warm blankets and Ben put the stocking cap back on him hoping his temperature would rise. Then he hung around to see what happened.

When the initial laboratory results were reported back, the resident came over to Ben and said, "Jeez, man. I've never seen this before," as he indicated a Blood Alcohol Concentration of greater than 0.3."

Ben said, "You're right. That's usually a death level for a guy this skinny. And what all are you doing?"

"The usual. I.V. fluid, pushing the glucose, I put a tube down to keep him from vomiting again, rinsed him out and put down a dose of activated charcoal and started a banana bag. Plus a dose of metadoxine."

"What's happening now?"

"His blood pressure is down to 80/50 and I think he's got Cheyne-Stokes," he said, referring to the abnormal breathing pattern that often precedes death in seriously ill patients.

"Crap. That's bad. It's time to play King Claudius," Ben said as he pulled out his phone and began looking through the numbers.

"What are you talking about?" asked the resident.

"King Claudius. In Hamlet. 'Diseases desperate grown, by desperate appliance are relieved, Or not at all.' "

"What the hell are you talking about?"

"I'm calling Donaldson. We need to get this guy on dialysis ASAP."

*   *   *

Fifteen minutes later Ben was scrubbing 'Barry's' belly in preparation for inserting a peritoneal dialysis catheter. His discussion with Jim Donaldson, the head of the Nephrology Division concluded that peritoneal dialysis could get started long before they could get vascular access and hemodialysis set up. Ben had completed the nephrology rotation the year before and knew how to insert the catheter. The ED nurses had been uneasy with the procedure and Ben spent time talking everybody through the steps while he was prepping the abdomen.

"While I'm getting this catheter in place, I want that two-liter bag of dialysate stuck in a blood warmer," he directed. "This guy is cool enough without me putting room temperature fluid in his belly."

In just minutes, the catheter was placed, tubing connected and two liters of warm dialysate was running into 'Barry's' belly. Almost as soon as the fluid finished its inward trip Ben was adjusting the tubing to allow the fluid to flow back out. He placed the empty bag on the floor and as it filled he directed the nurses to get another bag in the blood warmer for inflow.

"You're not leaving that fluid in very long," said the resident. "I thought the usual was at least two hour dwell time."

"Right," said Ben, not looking up. "But we're not doing dialysis for kidney disease. The alcohol molecule is small and will pass into the fluid very quickly. I bet the movement is almost complete by the time we let the two liters run in-that takes about twenty minutes, anyway."

Then the Emergency Head Nurse stuck her head in the door. "How long do you intend to keep that up?"

Ben answered, "Not sure, maybe a few hours."

"Then get him admitted and upstairs. I've got an Emergency area to run."

Ben grinned to himself and said, "Yes, m'am." Then he looked at the resident and jerked his head to indicate that the responsibility for admission was being passed to the more junior physician.

And so, when Jim Donaldson got the hospital to see his new consult, 'Barry' was in the Intensive Care Unit on his sixth peritoneal exchange. His blood pressure was 100/74 by then and his temperature was nearly 98 F. His most recent BAC was 0.22 and still dangerous but his breathing was near normal. And he was sound asleep.

CHAPTER 16

Saturday, November 2

The Medical Examiner arrived at the Grant home and had a short chat with Ron before starting her examination of the body. Gene slipped away and went upstairs while Ron decided to check out the kitchen. Gene came down the stairs a few minutes later and found Ron in the washroom off the kitchen.

"Looks like only one person slept in the bed, all right."

Ron didn't say anything but opened the lid on the washer to show Gene a gray sweatshirt in the tub with obvious black specks on it. As Gene nodded, Ron went over to the washtub and pointed to the pair of rubber gloves lying on the bottom. They both nodded and moved back into the dining room. The M.E. looked up at Ron and signaled by holding up her right hand with all fingers and thumb extended. -

Ron signaled Gene and they briefly talked off to the side. "I guess we are both in agreement that she was dead when the gun went off, right?" Ron said. Gene nodded in agreement. "Yeah, I saw the lividity on her back.

"It's there on her legs, too," Ron said. "I peeked under the chair."

"The Doc agrees. She's been dead for at least five hours."

"And not sitting in that chair most of that time."

"So, how do you see it, partner?" Gene asked. "I mean, I got my ideas but I want to hear yours."

Ron looked at his partner with a tenuous grin and said, "Well. Let's take the 'knowns' first. She's dead by about two a.m. and she lies on her back for at least three or four hours. Then she didn't get up and sit in the chair by herself."

"And she didn't pull the trigger on that shotgun, either," Gene added.

"So, if she's down and dead around two in the morning, it's likely from the 'spat' they had."

"No evidence of a big fight in here," Gene added, looking around the living room. "And no heavy objects."

"I checked on the way over here," Ron disclosed. "There's been no domestic disturbance calls for this address. So, if they fought before it was pretty quiet."

"Maybe this is the first time they came to blows."

"Yeah, could be. And let's say he hit her."

"She might have slapped him first."

"Could be, but we don't need that. If they're standing in the middle of the room and he hits her, what happens next?" Ron asks.

"She's not very big. A good blow would've knocked her down."

"What if she hit her head on that coffee table, then?

"Would that kill her?"

"Could have, maybe. If she hit her temple and cracked her skull, maybe."

"Whatever, we both agree she's down and dead by two. What's your thought about the shotgun?"

"I think he did that because she did have a head injury that caused death and he knew that would come out. With the shotgun and a 'suicide' her head injury would never be noticed." Ron says this with a slight flare of his nostrils. This story is becoming real to him and he doesn't like it.

"And you think it took him five hours to come up with that?"

"Yeah, 'cause he's not as smart as we are."

Gene nodded and went on, "But I think he needed a 'witness' and he couldn't get that until Bronsky went out for the paper."

"Yeah, That's good. He gets a 'witness' to hear the shot and to place him outside when it happens."

"Well, we agree that she's dead in the chair. So how does he fire the gun? The neighbor says he was at the door when it went off."

Ron shook his head a little. "The neighbor was looking at his paper. I think Steve, here, had everything rigged. Probably had the gloves right at the door, grabbed them and raced over to the gun while yelling. He pulls the trigger and races back to the front door. Yells at the neighbor and runs back in the house. Pulls off the sweatshirt and gloves and dumps them and gets blood on his shirt by holding her hand until the police arrive." By this point in the narrative, Ron is almost able to feel the events.

"So Bronsky thinks he was outside when the shot went off. And he dumps the sweatshirt because …?" Gene asks.

"It's got gunshot residue all over it. And if he was that close, the question would be how come he couldn't stop her?"

"Good story, and it fits the 'knowns'. And one other 'known' makes him one sick bastard."

"What's that?" asked Ron.

"He left her there and went upstairs and slept in the bed."

Ron walked slowly over to the grieving husband , stood him up and read him his rights and arrested him for the murder of his wife. Grant did not make any struggle and seemed to deflate when he heard the charge. The patrolman looked surprised but quickly took charge of the man and walked him out to the patrol car to drive him back to the station where Steven Grant would be formally charged.

It was mid-afternoon and they had already wrapped up a murder case.

"This may be our record, partner," Gene surmised. The medical examiner gave them a 'thumbs up' as she and the technicians put the body on a gurney. The two detectives stepped out onto the porch and reflexively looked toward their separate cars.

"Possibly so," Ron rejoined, thinking it was very likely he would not be late getting home.

"I think we should go have a beer," said Gene.

"That's not the smartest idea, we still have the rest of the shift to go."

"Let 'em call 'em in, we'll figger 'em out before dinner time. If we have to. I mean we took our turn in the rotation. And I still haven't had breakfast!"

"Yeah, right. Go get something to eat. I'll see you in the office. We've got enough paperwork on this one to last 'til dinner time."

CHAPTER 17

Monday, November 4

Ben walked into 'Barry's' room on the ward. After dialysis and the passage of twenty-four hours, 'Barry's' body temperature had recovered to normal and his blood alcohol level was low enough that medical personnel thought it safe for him to sleep it off on the ward and not encumber a bed in the ICU any longer. 'Barry' had been moved to the ward on Sunday afternoon. According to the chart, he spent a quiet afternoon and evening, snuggled in his bed except for eating meals.

Ben had snagged the bag of belongings from the emergency area while 'Barry' was being moved to the Intensive Care Unit and he now brought a clean T-shirt and some sweat pants left in the resident's call room for 'Barry' He had the backpack slung over his shoulder.

'Barry' was asleep but he had been awake earlier because the remains of breakfast sat on his bedside table. The dietician had suggested a full liquid diet but Ben thought 'Barry' had done that diet long enough and overrode the suggestion by ordering pancakes, syrup, sausage and a fruit cup. And two cups of coffee. A quick look at the tray indicated that 'Barry' did not much favor the fruit cup but everything else was eaten.

Ben laid his hand on 'Barry's' shoulder and said, "Barry, are you awake?"

"Mmm now," came a muffled reply.

"Can we talk?" Ben asked.

After several seconds, the old man rolled over on his back and looked at Ben. "Why?"

"Because I want to find out a couple of things."

"Why?" This was accompanied by eye closure.

"Come on. I'm your doctor and I want to make sure you get well."

"Why bother?"

"Mostly because that's what I do. But also because I'd like to know a couple of things in particular," Ben was using his most concerned voice but it did not look like it was registering with 'Barry'.

"Don' care."

"Look. Your lab values are a bit off and I'm giving you some sugar and some vitamins that will help your recovery but I would still like to know something more about you."

"Like what?' The eye opened a tiny bit but didn't look directly at Ben.

"Like, what is your name? We've been calling you 'Barry' but that's probably not your real name, is it?"

"I like Barry."

"Is that your name?" Ben sounded almost pleading as he asked.

"Barry." The eyes went closed again as 'Barry' nodded gently.

"All right, Barry. What's your last name?"

"Ne'er mind."

"OK, man. I get it. You want to play witness protection with me and that's fine. I don't need your real name to treat you."

"'K."

"Can you tell me about this?" Ben asked, holding up the whiskey bottle.

"What?" The eyes were still closed.

"This whiskey bottle." The eyes popped open and fixed on the bottle in Ben's hand. "Where did you get this?"

With eyes half-closed and darting around the room, 'Barry' said, "That's mine."

"I know that, 'Barry'. I found it in your backpack. What I want to know is where you got it."

"Why?"

"Because this is a very expensive whiskey. And it's very high alcohol content and that's probably why you damn near died drinking it, that's why. Where did you get it?" Ben's voice was getting louder and more harsh.

"It's mine. Gimme." 'Barry reached out for the bottle but Ben kept it out of reach.

"Look, I'll give you back the bottle when you leave the hospital but I really want to know how you got it," he said, assuringly. The two men looked steadily at each other for several seconds. Ben had the definite impression that 'Barry' was sizing him up to determine whether he was a truth-teller. The impression behind the intelligent eyes gave Ben a moment of pause. For that few seconds, it did not seem like the conversation was between the smart doctor and the alcohol ravaged man from the streets. Ben felt was talking to a comparable intellect and needed to up his game to make an impression. Then the moment faded, 'Barry's eyes seemed to unfocus.

"It's mine," 'Barry' said as he closed his eyes and turned on his side, terminating the interview.

"OK, buddy. I'll let you rest and recover. I'll be back tomorrow to talk again. Get your rest and have some eats." There was no response. "I'll see you tomorrow, then."

Ben went out to the nurses' station and made sure that a full diet was ordered for 'Barry' before he took the backpack and whisky bottle back to his office. As he put the backpack in his locker for safekeeping, Ben thought back to the intense interchange he had with 'Barry'. What was that flash in his eyes? Was 'Barry' playacting? Was he just trying to get a warm bed and a few good meals?

"Can't be it," Ben thought, "He was perilously close to death Saturday. I don't see him trying that just for a cot and some hots."

Before he clicked the lock in place on the locker, he had another fleeting thought. "Unless he was really trying to die."

CHAPTER 18

Tuesday, November 5

Ben and Susan had lunch together the next day. Sitting in the hospital cafeteria in a booth at the far end of the eating area, they attracted little attention. And that was perfectly fine with both of them. Like many hospital cafeterias, New City had opened their food service to some outside vendors while still providing some in-house cooking. The cafeteria offered one or two main dishes from the kitchen, such as lasagna or roasted chicken breast with three or four vegetable side dishes. The fast food area offered Chick-Fil-A and a local barbeque sandwich with French fried potatoes. The center of the area involved a very large salad bar featuring a wide selection of greens and garden offerings plus cold chicken or Tuna parts and six kinds of dressing. Drinks were available from water, tea and sodas to canned beverages of a selection of fruit flavors. And there was a soft ice cream dispenser. No one complained about the 'hospital food' at New City.

Susan had the hamburger patty without bun and some of the steamed vegetables while Ben's choice was the salad bar with chicken pieces and blue cheese dressing. They ate with little talk until they were almost finished and then Ben asked, "Was that unusual for there to be so few people in the ED on Saturday?"

"You know it's always unpredictable. What do they say, 'feast or famine?' But, yes, it was a little quiet. More than usual."

"I did a two-month rotation in Emergency during my internship."

"Here?"

"No. In Akron. The University here didn't have any rotating slots then and I wanted to 'do it all' before deciding on a residency." He emphasized the "do it all" with expansive movements of his hands and almost hit Susan's tea glass. "Whoops."

"How did that work out?" She asked, grabbing the glass and moving it away.

"Well, I was able to decide early on that I wasn't really cut out for surgery. There were some embarrassments. Let's say."

Susan laughed and said, "Oh, I have to know about this."

"Why? Can't we just forget that I mentioned it?"

"Not now, buster. Spill." She said this with a big grin, as she knew he wasn't really embarrassed or the subject would never have come up.

"It's all about the mask," Ben teased.

"You mean you want everyone to recognize you and give you credit?" she teased back.

"No. If that were the issue I could just put my name on the surgical cap. It's actually much simpler than that. Whenever I put on a surgical mask my nose immediately begins to itch. And, of course, if you're scrubbed in and got on sterile gloves, you can't do anything about it. Unless you want to rub your face on someone's sterile gown!"

"Oh no, you don't want to do that. But maybe you could get the circulating nurse to scratch it for you."

"Yeah, maybe. But that won't work for anything other than noses. And, even then, maybe only once during a given operation." Ben raised his eyebrows to indicate that his nose was not the only itchy part of his anatomy during surgical scrub. Susan looked appropriately shocked for the briefest of moments until she burst out laughing.

"But, did you like the ED?" She asked.

"Yes, I did. There was a lot of doing and I like that. Some of my best memories involve times in the ED and particular cases. I remember once a young woman came in the ED having grand mal seizures. The nurses and I got her on a bed and got something in her mouth and I didn't know what to do next. I had never seen someone with status epilepticus before. While I was standing there like a telephone pole, the head nurse appeared at my elbow with a syringe and asked, 'Do you want me to give her some phenobarb now, doctor?' I was able to nod, she made the injection and moments later the seizures stopped."

"The nurse to the rescue." Susan smiled

"Not the only time, either. I remember a kid, probably about fifteen who rode his bicycle right in front of an eighteen-wheeler on the highway. That kid was wide awake in the ED and had likely broken every bone in his body except his head bone."

"I've seen some of those, too. Tragic."

"One of the funniest cases I saw was during the holiday period and we were absolutely swamped. Every room full, people on carts in the hallways and a packed waiting area. I noticed this one guy in jeans and a leather jacket, leaning against the wall in the waiting area but he looked like he was waiting for someone, not a patient himself. But as we worked our way through the cases and things finally started to slow down, I noticed he was still there, leaning against the wall. There were seats available in the waiting area but he hadn't moved in a couple of hours. So, when I finished a case I was suturing I went over to him and said, "Are you waiting to be seen?"

He said, "Oh, I can wait 'til you've taken care of these emergencies."

I said, "What's wrong, I can help you now."

"Well," he said, "I've got my foreskin caught in my zipper."

Susan almost spilled her tea when she heard that. "And he didn't think that was an emergency?"

Ben answered solemnly, "I guess not."

"Pretty clearly you enjoyed your time in the ED."

"Mostly. But it just didn't give me any feedback."

"You mean follow-up."

"Exactly. Didn't know whether the wounds I closed healed well or the stomach pain resolved. No follow-up. And then I found internal medicine. Lots of mysteries, wide choice of possible treatments and total follow-up."

"And that's why you're here at New City?"

"True. This is one of the best young programs in the country. But now that I'm here there's an even better reason to stay." He said this with a shy grin flirting with her shamelessly.

Susan smiled back and said, "Weren't you going to check on 'Barry' after lunch?"

"Yes, I am. It's really bothering me how a homeless guy on the street ends up with a bottle of Bruichladdich X4 whiskey. That's got the highest proof of any whiskey available and a bottle like that costs close to $100."

"And you know this how?" Susan asked, surprised at the information and Ben's intensity.

"Back in college I worked in one of the ABC stores, mostly stocking and keeping inventory. Learned a fair amount about the drinking industry," he explained. "And my concern here is not just how he got his hands on it-it's the safety factor. This stuff in almost pure alcohol. Somebody like 'Barry' might be drinking it like cheap wine and get a belly full of enough alcohol to kill him."

"That's actually not theoretical in this case," she added. "He likely would have died if you hadn't dialyzed him."

Ben started to tell Susan about the conversation he had with 'Barry' that made him think the old man was more aware than they believed.

But Susan asked a question about peritoneal dialysis and they talked about that for the next few minutes. The urge to talk to her about his feeling about 'Barry' passed and Ben turned his attention to dessert.

Somewhat soberly they ate their desserts and tidied up their trays. Susan said she needed to get back to the ED so Ben took their trays to the tray-return area before he caught the elevator up to the ward. As he walked toward 'Barry's' room, Ben thought of a couple of different ways to approach getting 'Barry' to explain how he came to have a bottle of what was possibly the most expensive whiskey available. As he turned into the room, however, he realized the futility of his prior planning.

'Barry' was not in his bed. He had left the hospital.

CHAPTER 19

Monday, November 11

Ron and Gene stopped for lunch at a little sandwich shop near the station house. Ron liked the place because of their luncheon specials. Gene especially wanted to eat at this particular shop because he enjoyed watching a certain waitress as she moved through the business of getting orders and waiting on tables. The fact that this particular waitress, given name Sandra, was aware of Gene's attention made the episodes all that more attractive to Ron.

"Good day, Sandra," Ron said as she came to their table.

"Good afternoon, boys," she rejoined while not actually taking her eyes off Gene, who was watching her every move. He leaned back in the booth seat and said, "Good afternoon. I'll have my usual, Sandy."

"If you didn't, it wouldn't be 'usual' now would it?" She responded with her eyes and lips smiling.

"Let me have the triple cheese sandwich and fries," Ron said, feeling like he was talking to the side of her head.

"Right," she said without turning. "Iced tea like always?"

"Sure, honey," Gene said.

Ron tried to get her attention by nodding but she turned and walked away as if she knew he had agreed with her suggestion. And he and Gene admired her going away.

"Are you ever going to ask her out?" Ron inquired, reaching for the napkins.

"Ah, you know," Gene pondered, "I might just spoil these enjoyable lunches."

"Or you might add on some enjoyable dinners, or movies, or whatnot."

"It's the whatnot that keeps me from trying," Gene said, brightly.

"Oh come on, Gene. She's obviously noticed your interest and is signaling back."

"We've talked this over before. I'm not seeing it that way. Maybe she's angling for better tips. Although she does make more trips to our table than to others … "

"And she knows what your 'usual' is. I doubt she knows whether I want sweet tea or not. And I am a little tired of being ignored when you're at the table."

"It's the suit, man. If you didn't dress like a married man on a cops' budget you might get more attention, too."

"I get all the attention I want-or need-at home. Thank you very much," Ron said.

"Whatever. I'm still basking in the glow from that case last week. Five hours and a solved murder. Maybe we should get medals or something."

"That's gonna happen. I heard the brass was planning a ceremony for us at City Hall; big band and all that. Mayor's gonna speak."

"I may need a new suit."

"The one you're wearing doesn't look like it's been off the rack more than a day. You have how many suits, now?"

"Enough, actually. But the ties, now I could use a new tie."

Ron snorted and said, "Bud, you show up in a new tie every day. You can't need a new one."

"It's to celebrate. I like to get a new tie whenever there's a reason to celebrate."

"You must celebrate getting back home every night because I don't think I have ever seen you wear a tie the second time."

"Rumors. Speaking of rumors, what about the idea that the brass is getting serious about everyone getting the flu shot?"

"They are serious. Not a rumor. Remember last year when we operated at half-staff for a month? My buddy, Tom Bolling, over at New City said the damn flu bug mutated and nobody's vaccine worked."

"So, why bother if it's likely to happen again?"

"That was supposed to be the outlier. Not likely to happen again. We should get the shots soon because the flu season is about to begin."

"Not me. I'm gonna wait it out. Just like last year."

"Unless the brass catches you."

"Are they checking our shot records, now?"

"You never know. That reminds me of a story Tom Bolling told me. There was this base where the shot clinic was only getting about 10% mission completion of their routine immunizations. So this GMO cooks up a scheme and takes an ambulance and medics out to the individual squadrons, one each day on a two-month rotation and catches everyone who needs a shot when they sign up for muster. Got nearly 100% completion and won a Commendation."

"Yeah, I don't see Thor coming around to our desk every month to check our shots."

"No, but he might send somebody. Or catch you when you get sick."

"Don't let him get to talking with Tom, then."

"Here's your lunch, boys," said Sandra putting the plates in front of them and setting out their glasses of tea.

Later when they finished eating, Ron went to get his car and left Gene talking with Sandra. He pulled up in front of the shop a few minutes later but still had to wait several minutes for Gene to leave and come to the car.

"Long discussion there, partner," Ron suggested.

"Wrangling over the tip."

"She want to wrassle you for it?

"I was defending your small offering."

CHAPTER 20

Monday, November 18

Tom Bolling pulled his F-150 into the New City parking garage and into his allotted space. As he set the parking brake he realized he had only thought about two issues on the way to the hospital that morning. He considered it unusual for him not to have five or more things to consider on the ride to the hospital. But this time he had spent his drive thinking mostly about the divide within New City over the academic affiliation.

Tom knew the history of the hospital and its origin as the Railway Hospital intended for the employees and families of the rail lines serving the city. Having studied the history of American medicine, Tom knew that such facilities and others in early logging communities were among the first types of 'pre-paid' health insurance. And he understood the change wrought in society by WWII and how the post-war period included expanded capabilities and ever more expanding expectations for the medical community.

Railway Hospital had been 'updated' with city funding in the early 1950s but still had not been considered 'first-tier' care. Only after Regents Incorporated purchased the facility and turned to for-profit care did the hospital begin to draw favorable reviews. As a for-profit hospital, and not the only one in the Greater Cincinnati area, New City had overcome its image as being 'on the wrong side of the tracks' starting with its endorsement of Medicare. By the time the rest of the medical community adopted methods to encompass Medicare patients, New City had reached outside the Cincinnati catchment area, enhanced its open heart surgery program and used new federal capital to add shiny buildings to their growing reputation of shiny technology.

When the academic affiliation with South West Ohio Medical School was introduced, practicing physicians initially endorsed the activity with a belief that the students and residents would enhance their income by allowing more patients to be seen. Their involvement in the teaching and supervision aspects of the affiliation was seen as a distraction from income generation, however, and had been a source of sparks and even fire at times. Tom was aware that the two previous chiefs of staff at New City were seen as unsuccessful because they could not bridge that divide.

The 'solution', developed over years of hiring faculty-approved physicians as full-time at New City with regular teaching responsibilities, was finally coming to be seen as progress. Tom had worried a little about the culture clash before taking the job. Now he wondered if he should have worried more. The recent conversation with Dick Abert had remained in his subconscious and Tom had thought of several different ways he might have framed the discussion so it would have been better received. Dick was a university recommended hire and he brought expertise and reputation as a nationally renowned endocrinologist to New City. Dick didn't want much to do with the 'business' of medicine, a mirror imager of the previous generation of New City physicians who wanted little do to with the 'teaching' of medicine.

On the trip in to New City, Tom had also thought about the rewarding Grand Rounds that Ben Nealy and George Hacker had put together for the students and physician staff and faculty. Making that diagnosis was insightful and resourceful on Ben's part but it was probable that other physicians might also have figured out the sequence and become suspicious of poisoning. But the academic and scholarly thought that then went into constructing a teaching program was what gave Tom a warm feeling and a strong argument to continue his fight for strengthening the affiliation.

Somewhat buoyed by those last thoughts, Tom exited his truck and started toward the door. He slowed his approach to correspond to the pace of another physician entering the hospital.

"Good morning, Ike. Did I hear something about you having a lot of leftover candy from Halloween?"

Isaac Wallenberger was the chief of general surgery and assistant chief of the department. He was a striking individual of almost six feet in height, very broad of shoulder and notable for the complete absence of hair on his head. One could tell he shaved his head but the effect was an almost luminous white sphere with small eyes, insignificant nose and thin lips. Another notable thing about Ike was that he walked to the hospital every day from his home slightly more than two miles away.

"Hey, General. That rumor bothered me so I ate it all. None left."

"Well, I'll try again next year."

"Better up your game to asking on the first of November, then."

"Good idea," Tom said following Ike into the lobby and winking at Nick.

CHAPTER 21

Saturday, December 21

That Saturday started off as a typical one in the Emergency area at New City. All the camaraderie from Thanksgiving had been dispelled and the tryptophan-induced sleepiness had been overcome. People were back on the road and banging into each other or taking too much self-medication either from home or a local bar. And many of them then ended up in one of the rooms in the New City Emergency Department.

Around four o'clock, on their second delivery of the day, police officers helped move a wiry old man from the back seat of their cruiser to a gurney and accompanied him and the orderlies into the ED.

"Junkie," said the older officer. "Found him down in the alley downtown. Looks like he OD'd. Responded to one dose of Narcan and came up swinging, so we brought him in. Maybe you can calm him down."

The old man was dressed in dirty pants, an even dirtier shirt and worn-out house slippers. His hair was long and dirty and he lay twitching on the gurney and mumbling with occasional loud shouts. The nurses took him into a room and tried to help him move from the gurney to a bed but he was not willing to move. He fought against them until the police went into the room and assisted in the move by overpowering the old man and shifting him into the bed where the nurses restrained him. The Emergency resident was unable to get a name or a complaint from the old man and so he started the discussion about disposition.

Susan Chang had been in the back of the ED with another patient but was asked to join the conversation about what to do with the vagrant.

"What's the deal?" she asked.

"He's drugged up and out of it and doesn't really have a medical problem we should admit," said one of the other nurses.

"You could make an Observation patient until tomorrow morning," the social worker suggested to the resident.

Susan balked at that idea saying, ""That's just pushing the work off on the nurses. We would have to watch him closely even in Observation. What do we know about him? Any ID?" She went into the room to see how disoriented the man was. Susan quickly went through his pockets but discovered no further information. The resident came to the other side of the bed and said, "I'm really not comfortable sending this guy back out of the street. Cops said he was dosed up."

The old man said, "Whaaa?" and rolled over on his back. The long hair fell away from his face and Susan said, "Ohmigod, that's 'Barry'".

She told the other nurses that the patient would almost certainly be admitted and went to the phone to call Ben Nealy.

Ben happened to be on call and was in the library reading the last week's journals when his phone rang.

"Hey, Suse. I was about to call and see if we could do dinner together."

Susan's end of the conversation was being watched by the other nurses and so she responded somewhat more formally with, "Dr. Nealy, there's a patient in the Emergency area that I believe you know and we would like some assistance with his disposition?"

"What? Oh, they're listening aren't they?"

"Yes."

"Who is it?"

"I believe it's the man 'Barry' who was here several weeks ago."

"Really? He's back? What happened?"

"The police found him with a drug overdose."

"I'm on my way. Don't let him leave like he did before."

"He will not be going anywhere, I promise."

The library was on the second floor and Ben did not wait for the elevator, taking the steps two at a time and hustled down the back hallway. He didn't slow down until just before hitting the back door into the Emergency area. Then he took a deep breath and calmly pushed open the door and walked toward the nurses' station.

Susan indicated which room he wanted and walked to the doorway as Ben went up to the bedside.

"Hey, buddy. 'Barry'. Its' Doctor Nealy. Let's get you comfortable, OK?" Ben brushed the hair out of 'Barry's' face and adjusted the pillow under his head. Then, smiling at 'Barry' like a long lost friend he said, "What's going on 'Barry'?"

"Stupid," 'Barry' slurred.

"Where did you get the dope, 'Barry'?"

"Dint," the old man slurred and again tried to turn on his side. Ben let him turn and quickly checked over 'Barry's' arms. "No tracks," he said, as much to himself as to anyone else. By this time the emergency resident had joined him in the room and asked, "You know this guy?"

"Yeah. He and I did a little dialysis dance a few weeks ago and then he went AMA."

"He's a dialysis patient?"

"No. No, He was just super drunk."

"Oh yeah. I heard about that."

"I guess we were the talk of the town for a few days. And now, here he is with a near fatal drug overdose-and apparently the first time he tried it."

"What do you mean?" asked the resident.

"He has no needle tracks anywhere on him. Look for yourself." They did, looking at both arms and legs and between his toes. They found ground in dirt and plenty of scratches and even an open wound on his buttock. But there were no signs of previous intravenous drug use.

By the time they had finished examining 'Barry', the subject of all this attention was somewhat more awake. "Cha doin?" He mumbled at the resident while trying to bat away his hand.

Ben tried to soothe 'Barry' by saying, "We're just making sure everything is OK with you, buddy." Then he turned to the resident and said, "Let's get him admitted. Put him up on my ward."

"Diagnosis?"

"Try illegal substance overdose and withdrawal."

"Suits me. The Head Nurse will be pushing for him to be gone."

"You mean Nurse Ratchett? Just tell her that he's going to my team. She'll think that's appropriate."

"No. I mean Ms. Swilling."

"That's who I mean, too," said Ben. "Ratchett." Turning back to 'Barry', Ben said, "Welcome, back, Barry. Looks like we're getting the band back together."

CHAPTER 22

Sunday, December 22

'Barry' had a quiet night. After Ben wrote the orders and had him admitted to the ward, there was that short period of time where he had time without someone asking him questions or seeing to his care. His blood pressure was measured along with his blood oxygen level and he was assisted into some hospital pajamas. Other than those medical interruptions, 'Barry' slept throughout the night. Ben looked in on him early when he came for rounds on the ward. When he had finished his own daily work he returned back to 'Barry's' room. He quietly shook 'Barry' to wake him up and then sat on the bed next to him and talked about what happened with the needle.

Ben started by asking, "Look, 'Barry', I know you're not a drug addict. So how did you get a dose of heroin?"

"Din't," was the reply.

"Did someone give you the drugs, 'Barry'?"

"S'pect so."

"Really? That's good to know, 'Barry'. Do you know who it was?"

"Unh uh."

"What? Who was it?"

"G'way"

"Barry," Ben asked patiently, "what is your name? I'd really like to address you correctly. Tell me you name and I'll tell you mine. Please?"

"Don know," was the slurred answer.

Ben had some experience in dealing with drunks and addicts and somehow was convinced the confusion and difficulty in communicating he was having with 'Barry' had little to do with either of those situations. 'Barry' appeared at times to be well aware of Ben's questions and seemed to dodge them intentionally. Ben began to think perhaps 'Barry' didn't really remember anything about that needle but was fearful if he convinced people he didn't know what happened they might put him back on the street.

Yet, through all the grime and unkemptness, Ben felt a sense of cognizance in the old man and a true reticence for sharing his background and story. So he allowed him to sleep and mumble and not answer questions. Instinctively, Ben thought the man's name might have a clue to what was driving his secretiveness. And that was turning out to be the mountain he couldn't climb.

"Listen, 'Barry', he said, "I'm going to let you sleep. I remember you did pretty well with the diet you had last time so I've ordered that again. I'll come by and talk with you again around breakfast time in the morning."

'Barry's' response was to snuggle into his pillow.

"Before I leave, is there anything else I can get you? Anything you need?"

"Whiskey?"

"Well, anything other than that. You and I still have some discussion pending about that bottle you left behind, right?"

"'S mine."

"So it is, 'Barry', so it is. I still have it and we can talk tomorrow about you having it back. OK?"

"K"

"All right, then. See you for breakfast."

Ben left and slowly walked to area with the call rooms and individual resident lockers. 'Barry's' circumstance was again a puzzling one for him. Old guy, out on the street, no obvious money or support and a clear affinity for booze but not for drugs. Yet he now shows up with street drug overdose. And no other track marks. What makes a guy go from zero to 100 miles an hour on intravenous drugs? Just as with the whiskey, a serious question was 'how did he pay for drugs on the street?' and Ben had no immediate answer.

Perhaps the old guy was subconsciously suicidal. Circumstance on the street, sleeping in alleys, picking through garbage cans for food and panhandling were not examples of living the high life. Ben could understand depression and, maybe, even thoughts of suicide. But there were cheaper ways to kill yourself than what 'Barry' had gotten into. Jumping off a bridge or stepping in front of a bus would end things pretty quickly with no out of pocket requirement.

Ben thought about whether this man might have some secret cache of money he could tap, not enough for regular food and shelter but enough to make the exit from a miserable life more comfortable than a bone-crushing event. That raised more questions. Where was that cache? How did he access it? Where did he get that money in the first place?

Such thinking pushed Ben back to the question of why 'Barry' was so reticent about giving them his name. Was his name the key to what was going on? Perhaps he had been in witness protection and his drinking made him forget his secret identity. Or he was on the run from the drug gangs. Actually, Ben thought, that's really far-fetched since he had no affinity for drugs. Ben wondered what Susan would think about 'Barry' and the possibility that he might have known the person who gave him the heroin injection. She always seemed to have good theories about people.

As he lay on the couch in the call area thinking about this, Ben became convinced there must be some serious concern 'Barry' had for the future, or maybe from the past, to push him to act like this. What could the old guy have gotten into? Was he running from something? Or was somebody chasing him?

CHAPTER 23

Monday, December 23

"Back again, Ben?" said Angie, secretary to Dr. Richard Abert, Chairman of Medicine at New City.

"Yes, I am. Can't stay away from these marvelous brownies," Ben said as he chose one from the plate on Angie's desk. "I think I'll sit here and eat the whole plate." He sat down in one of the chairs by the door and smiled at her.

"You know, he told me you'd be coming back," Angie smiled at him. "And he said to let him know when you got here."

"He said after lunch but he didn't clarify if that was after my lunch or his. But I've eaten."

"He just came back with a sandwich. He's attending this month and the days get later a little sooner if you understand."

"Sure do. That's my day, too. It's OK. I'll be quiet over here," he said as he leaned his head back against the wall and closed his eyes.

Ben thought back to the earlier conversation he had with Dr. Abert. He had been on call on Saturday and was one of the residents of record at the Monday morning report with the Chairman. He and the other resident and two interns who had fielded the admissions and provided on-call services for patients throughout the hospital during the night sat in the Chairman's office to report on what happened during that time. Morning report had many functions, Ben supposed, but he was primarily interested in the function of it being over.

The Chairman had other ideas and he was the one in charge so Ben's goal had to wait. The interns quickly presented each new admission using the "30 second" format. This brief presentation provided the Chair with the age, sex, chief complaint, major findings and presumed diagnosis in bullet format for each patient. Longer presentations with greater detail, including pertinent negatives about things not found or complained of were reserved for different settings. Fortunately for Ben there were only four admissions and all were fairly straightforward, even 'Barry', up to a point. Nonetheless the Chairman used the opportunity to emphasize his favorite function of Morning Report by making each case a teaching moment. He quizzed the interns about their understanding of the deranged physiology of each diagnosis and the approved first line of treatment.

Ben had spent 30 minutes with the interns before Report going over each of the cases with this paradigm in mind. He 'pimped' them on the questions that would be asked and drilled them on providing succinct answers. He had sat in the Report session, half listening to the answers the interns were giving and half thinking about the conversation he needed to have with the chairman when the Report was over. Ben knew the interns were just as interested as Ben to get the Report over and done quickly. The Christmas to New Year period was 'holiday time' for trainees. Over the ten day period they each worked five days at double-time covering for someone who was 'on holiday' so they could have the other five days off themselves. They were looking at a full day of double responsibility and they wanted to get to it.

As the Report finally ended and the Chairman said, "Merry Christmas", the interns got up and quickly left but Ben remained in his chair. "Sir," he said, "I need to talk to you about something that is troubling me."

Thereafter he and the chairman had talked about his concerns for the next 20 minutes. Ben used the "three minute" presentation to provide background on 'Barry'-at least what little they knew: probable age, sex, and circumstances of the original encounter plus the clinical and laboratory findings at the current admission. The chairman indicated that he was aware of the dialysis process in the Emergency area but that the height of the blood alcohol level had not been mentioned. Ben had pressed on, explaining that his concern centered on how a destitute and homeless old guy got his hands on a bottle of Bruichladdich X4. There had been a short detour to talk about the Bruichladdich since the chairman had not heard of it before but then he had expressed the same wonder at 'Barry's' possession of it. At that point in the presentation Ben shifted to 'Barry's' second admission with a near fatal intravenous drug overdose. The chairman had seemed puzzled about the import of this until Ben noted his previous and current physical examinations had not noted any evidence of previous intravenous drug use.

At that point, Ben made his startling claim, "I think somebody is trying to kill this man." That comment had clearly taken Dr. Abert back a bit. He had then admitted there were some odd circumstances surrounding each of the medical encounters but did not think there was enough to make a solid case. When Ben countered that the proximity in time and the severity of the oddities surely made a connection, the chairman had replied, "Two points make a line, Ben. It takes at least three to make a trend."

At that point Ben's response had expressed more irritation than reason and he had then argued the third time might be a success. He also noted that if it was a success that he and New City would not be notified. That comment had initially puzzled the Chairman and he asked for clarification. Ben had explained that if the police found 'Barry' dead on the street the coroner would be the one who got to see what might then just look like 'a first time'. The chairman had indicated that he was not suggesting they wait for a third time, only that the case needed strengthening.

Ben's suggestion then was for the chairman to ask Dr. Bolling to get his friend that cleared up the cardiology case to take on the task of getting more information. Dr. Abert had not not particularly keen about involving police but he did see some merit in Ben's idea. However, he did not want to be presenting the chief of staff with a potential crime scenario solely on hearsay. He told Ben he would arrange for the two of them to meet with Tom but only after he, the chairman, had a chance to talk to 'Barry' and look at his arms. Abert had attending responsibilities, however, and needed to get off to the wards. They had agreed to meet back at his office "after lunch" to go visit 'Barry'.

Accordingly Ben kept his promise to 'Barry' and accompanied his breakfast tray into the room. Noting that 'Barry' was awake he said, "Ready for breakfast, aren't you?" he had said, swinging the overbed tray into position so 'Barry' could eat sitting in the bed. Then he had taken a position in a chair next to bed and again tried to get information from the old man.

"Will you tell me your name?" he had asked.

'Barry' hadn't replied but put a bite of pancake in his mouth and shook his head.

"Is there some reason you need to keep your identity secret?" Ben persisted.

"Don know," 'Barry' had slurred through another large bite of food.

"I'll keep it secret if you tell me, I promise," Ben then promised.

"You got my whiskey," was the reply. Not a question, a statement.

"And I have kept it safe," Ben had nodded. "I will give it back when you are ready to leave the hospital, OK?"

No response. More eating. Ben had watched and waited for 'Barry' to initiate conversation. That had not happened.

"Look, I can't give it to you while you are a patient in here," Ben had explained more quietly. "How about if I bring it by later and let you see it, so you'll know it's safe with me? Would you tell me what's going on and what your name is then?"

"Maybe," came a grudging answer as 'Barry' wiped the last of the syrup up with the final bit of pancake.

"OK, my friend. That's good enough for me." Ben rose from the chair and started toward the door. "Oh, by the way, right after lunch I'm going to bring a friend around to see you and talk with you. A real smart doctor. You want some more coffee?"

Ben had asked the nurse to get 'Barry' a second cup of coffee and then went to take care of his own morning work which included getting his team ready for attending rounds of their own.

Ben sat there thinking two thoughts simultaneously, "This chair is not very comfortable" and "It's after my lunch," when the door to the chairman's office opened and Dr. Abert stuck out his head. "Be right there, Ben," he said before the door closed.

"I told him you were waiting," Angie reported to his puzzled look.

"Of course you did. I think I'll just have another brownie."

"And here we all thought you were finished with lunch," she said lifting the plate toward him.

"Oh, I am. This is … dessert. Or a snack. Whatever. They are so good!"

Barely three minutes later Dr. Abert came out of his office, putting on his white coat as he did. "Let's go see your fellow," he said to Ben. He had a few questions for Ben as they walked over to the ward but once again Ben's desire to get to the bottom of 'Barry's' mystery was thwarted by one simple act. 'Barry' was not in his bed. The nurses on the ward indicated that he had left the hospital again.

CHAPTER 24

Monday, December 23

One of the traditions at New City, and likely at most every hospital, is the informal competition around each ward's individual Christmas 'Party'. Some were more elaborate with wall and ceiling hangings of crepe paper and paper bells while others were renowned for their awesome array and delicious choices of candies and sweets. And, each ward had a reputation regarding their singular drink for the occasion. Most had a cold punch, some with decorated miniature ice carvings floating in an ornate bowl; others went for mulled cider or a spicy cinnamon tea. The usual smells of hospital care, alcohol, antiseptic, and powder, were supplanted by the fragrance of spices and the smell of freshly baked goods. It was a wonderful time to walk around the hospital.

Tom Bolling had created a tradition of making that walk during the holiday season. Every day he visited several of the wards and treatment areas between 10:30 and 1:00 in the afternoon. He became the guest of honor at each gathering and easily allowed himself to be tempted with party sandwiches, brownies, and beverages all the while wondering out loud if "this may be the best ward party in the hospital."

Tom's second visit was to the Operating Room area where the nurses had decorated the recovery area and laid out some of Tom's favorite food-pimento cheese sandwiches. A surgeon himself, Tom thought of the OR staff, including the recovery room personnel, as his kind of people. The surgical nurses were, in his opinion, just a little more focused on getting the right thing done at exactly the right time. Once the skin incision is made during surgery, surgeons expect that the sequence of events will proceed in a predictable manner to shorten the time of anesthesia. This expectation extended to any request for a surgical instrument and their belief that it will be ready for them. They are so aware of the way things should go that their dictated notes after surgery repeatedly mention that things were done "in the usual fashion" often without further explanation.

Tom's arrival in the preparation area of the operating room was greeted by huzzahs from the group of nurses gathered there. Just as he thought of them as his kind of people, the operating room staff considered him to be their kind of chief of staff. Although Tom had not obtained privileges for surgery at New City, the nursing staff had done their due diligence in researching his background before he arrived.

His time in Balad taught Tom that "the usual fashion" often was quite unusual in times of disaster. He knew trauma teams many times reverted back to basics like gross anatomy during times of 'Where's that damn artery supposed to be?" and the "usual' fashion was something no one in the room had ever seen or done before. It was that flexibility and responsiveness that he had seen so often in wartime that made him think most highly of the OR nursing staff.

"Dr. Bolling," one of the scrub nurses said loudly. "We've got your pimento cheese sandwiches right here."

"My favorite!" he responded, grabbing one of the half-sandwiches off the tray and maneuvering himself toward the hot tea dispenser.

After one cup of tea, a half sandwich and a cracker with cream cheese and pepper jelly, Tom asked for everyone's attention. In the previous year he had noted what he considered long turn-around times between operations and had brought that to the attention of the Head Nurse in the OR. His own experience in Balad had been that such turn-around could be accomplished in about half the time. Initially nursing was not convinced that there could be much improvement in the time and had reluctantly agreed to create a team to examine whether improvement was possible.

Tom spoke to that history, saying, "I know y'all were not enthused about my suggestion that we could improve our turn-around time."

There was good-natured laughter and smiles all around in response.

"But I also know that you spent time in good faith studying the possibility."

This was followed by some serious head nodding.

"And you know what your efforts produced. A forty percent reduction in turn-around time, an increase of nearly 12 operations a week and a significant increase in the hospital income from this area!"

This time his comments were followed by applause.

Tom went on to mention that he was aware of the time they had spent working on reducing the turn-around time for the ORs. He said they had done great work and he was very proud of them and got a second round of applause. What he didn't say was he knew that the team responsible for the new process included members of the housekeeping crew that mopped the floor. The initial team composed only of nurses made virtually no progress until they had added the housekeepers to the team. Tom felt that lesson on team membership was as important as the improvement in the turn-around time. He left the area with many comments of good cheer and headed for the Emergency Department.

Again, his entrance was greeted with cheers; everyone knew what his visit would entail. Tom liked to use the spirit of the time to make his visits encouraging and special. In the nurses' station in the Emergency area, his annual visit coincided with an award for the intern who, in the first six months of their career, had been the most parsimonious with the use of suture material. This award, The Scotch

Trophy, also presented in June to a second winner was comprised of a labeled, spring-loaded clothespin to which was glued a dispenser of Scotch brand clear tape.

Tom made a big show of having consulted with numerous individuals before recognizing the winner. Part of his fun was bringing up particular events in the ED that had become common knowledge and that involved one or more interns. Last year, he had made mention of the "B.O.W. Incident" wherein one of the interns was seeing a woman in the ED who was in labor when her water broke. The intern, fearing a delivery in the ED, shoved the bed containing his patient into the hall and raced with it toward the elevators. All might have been well had they not clipped the hallway water fountain, which knocked it completely loose and flooded the entire area. That earned a Bag of Waters award and an impassioned speech from Tom saying he did not want to ever have to award that kind of activity again.

After making some amusing comments about the fumblings of various interns in the ED, he announced the First Six Month winner of the Scotch Award-Mary Jane Blessing. As Mary Jane came to accept her prize, the Head Nurse, Ms. Edna Swilling said, quite loudly, "This one is the best ever with that 3-0 thread." That got a big laugh from everyone. Mary Jane didn't have to give an acceptance speech so everyone moved into the backroom for punch and cookies.

Later, while Mary Jane was holding court on how to do instrument ties and leave only short ears, Ms. Swilling edged next to Tom, standing at the periphery of the crowd. "He's a little better. But it happened again last week."

"Dandrige?"

"Yes. You could smell it on him but he acted sober and calm. I wasn't here but the girls told me. I would have made him leave. But they said he talked to the kid and the family and no one raised an eyebrow."

"They probably thought we just pulled him away from dinner and a glass of wine," said Tom. "People give their physician a lot of rope."

"He's been in since. No hint of drinking. And no breath mints or anything like a cover-up."

"You know I had a talk with him," Tom said glancing sideways to assure they were not being overheard.

"I know. You told me. But I said I'd keep watching and let you know."

"I appreciate that, Edna. Merry Christmas." The nurse eased away and fell into conversation with one of the interns.

Tom finished his cup of punch and looked at his watch. Only 12:30. He headed for the stairs thinking he had time to get to one more ward party before his afternoon meeting.

CHAPTER 25

Monday, December 23

Mary Brighthouse looked up as the two doctors entered the office of the chief of staff.

"Dr. Abert, how are you?" she said as she picked up the phone to tell Tom that his visitors had arrived. Tom had offered her time off for the holiday but she had decided that she would rather have a few days later in the year for her son's fortieth birthday. She brushed some gray hairs back over her ears and said, "Is everyone in Medicine enjoying their holidays?"

"I think so," answered Abert. "And, by the way, this meeting is likely to be shorter than I thought."

'That's OK. He has already made his 'Party Rounds' and has nothing scheduled for the rest of the day."

"Mastone out for the holiday?" asked Abert.

"No. But he's pretty much out of the building. Parties with the downtown brass and like that," she said with just a touch of dismissiveness. Abert knew how much Tom relied on Mary's insight into people and politics of the hospital so he took a chance by asking, "Tom OK about the cardiology mess?"

Mary smiled her gentle little smile and replied, "He has that situation in control. Gave it right back to them to work out the details."

"Exactly right," Abert nodded. "They kept trying to go around me and get him to do their work. I'm glad he stopped them."

Ben stood quietly listening to this line of inside gossip. He knew all about the recent deaths and the vacancies in Cardiology; those events and the involvement of Bolling's detective friend was exactly why he thought getting Dr. Bolling involved-along with his old friend the homicide detective-would be useful in working through what he was positive involved attempted murder embroiling 'Barry'. However, he was fairly certain that he was not supposed to be over hearing the gossip about interpersonal friction among the physician faculty so he tried to look like he wasn't listening. It occurred to him that he could best appear so by focusing on his phone. He took it out and started reading some texts from earlier in the day.

Mary and Abert did not seem to notice Ben's presence but shifted the content of their discussion to more general topics. "Got all the shopping done?" Mary asked.

"Shopping, yes. Wrapping, no. In fact, I'm a little concerned that I may not remember where everything is hidden."

"That's why I wrap them up as soon as I get them in the house," Mary said smartly. "One year I forgot a fancy pen I had for my daughter-in-law. She was aware that her presents were fewer than others had. And I didn't connect until my son, said something about 'we still love you' that I realized what happened."

"Good times," Abert said, sarcastically.

"Come in, Tom said from his open doorway. They entered the office with Abert leading but he immediately stepped back and indicated that Ben had asked for the meeting and would start the discussion.

Ben made his three minute presentation before he explained that the man had left the hospital AMA and that Abert did not have opportunity to confirm the findings Ben described. Following his brief presentation, Tom and Abert were silent.

Ben felt he was being left on his own in the argument so he stepped up his presentation. "Look, sir, this is all my idea. I'm just concerned about the appearances. Here's a guy that probably can't afford a bottle of Three Buck Chuck and somehow he gets a bottle of 180-proof whiskey and promptly drinks himself near death. Even though we bail him out, he acts like he's in the witness protection program. Won't tell us his name or anything about himself. Checked out AMA and then a few weeks later he's back with a heroin overdose. This is a guy who never used intravenous drugs before. I mean he has no track marks, no history. That's got to raise some eyebrows, right?"

Tom raised his hand and said, "Look Ben, I don't think Dick is saying you are wrong. But the guy is gone and we don't have any proof of wrong-doing here. I don't know what we could do at this point, anyway. You pointed out that he is homeless so we have no address to go find him, isn't that correct?"

"Yes, sir. That's right. But the police have found him twice in the same area and we do know where that is."

"But we don't have the authority to go pick people up off the street. We provide care when they are brought to us but we aren't allowed to go sweeping them up."

"Maybe not, sir. I mean I understand your argument from a public health perspective but this is just one guy. I'm not advocating a general sweep of the area."

"And for what reason would we bring this man back to the hospital, Ben? We have no proof of malfeasance here and from what you say the guy is pretty unhelpful himself."

"What kind of proof could there be better than 180-proof whiskey to a drunk or intravenous dosing to a non-user to suggest that something is rotten here?"

"Ben, I know you had a good pick-up with that farmer last year but, really, not every bizarre set of circumstances points to attempted murder!"

"You think I'm making this up, Dr. Bolling? These are not suppositions. Every thing I mentioned is a fact. He had the whiskey bottle. He had the overdose and only the fact that the patrol officers carry Narcan kept him alive."

Abert inserted, "We talked about before and agreed that two times is not a trend, Ben."

"And we also said that the third time might be the end, too," Ben said, losing a little steam as he realized he had no stronger arguments and the ones he had were not persuasive. He looked back and forth between the two senior physicians and sighed deeply.

"Come on fellows," Tom said, getting up and walking them to the door. "There's nothing we can do now, anyway since our patient of concern has left the building. Ben, I promise you that if he turns up again, I'll go see him with you to see if we can straighten this out, OK?"

Ben nodded his agreement and Tom said, "Merry Christmas," as they left the office.

CHAPTER 26

Monday, December 23

Tom Bolling's Christmas Party for the Faculty at New City was always a big favorite. When he announced the party the first year after he had accepted the position as chief of staff, the opinion across the faculty was this was a 'must show' affair. The General was holding a party and, no matter how dull and boring, it was expected that each and every member would show their face. After a decent interval they expected to excuse themselves and get away to a more enjoyable evening somewhere else - anywhere else.

Five years later and the Bolling's party was one of the most looked-forward-to events of the year. Right up there with Match Day. And everyone knew the party's success was almost entirely due to Sandra's planning, menu and careful attention to detail. The house was decorated tastefully but minimally, and there were snacks, hors d'oeurves, cheeses, dips, and desserts abounding all over the house. But the center of attention was traditionally the same. Tom arranged in the center of the dining room table a spiral-sliced peppered ham from Arkansas. Plus Sandra arranged a series of trays containing biscuits, rolls, crackers and pita breads to handle the ham. Last, there were the condiments, two German mustards, a Dijon-flavored one, mayonnaise and Tom's homemade horseradish-in-whipped cream. Even though the

Bolling's took care to insure adequate seating throughout the house it always seemed the dining room was crowded especially around the ham and whipped cream end of the table.

Children were welcomed with their own room of goodies and DVDs of favorite children's Christmas movies. Some of the children favored the ham as much as the adults; others were drawn, over and over, to fill their plate with the brined shrimp.

Perhaps the most interesting part of the party was the absence of strong drink. Or beer. Red or white wine was available on the kitchen bar along with an array on non-alcoholic drinks: sodas, lemonade, coffee, hot or iced tea, mulled cider and what the chief of surgery called 'diet water', unsweetened flavored water. And no one left early, it seemed. Some actually came early if they had a competing event but most everyone was present within 10-15 minutes of the announced start time and stayed throughout. Sandra cleverly arranged to preclude the likelihood of long-staying guests by setting both a starting time and an ending time for the party on the invitations.

For several years Tom had invited Ron and Meg to attend as well. They found it easy to associate with many of the hospital faculty and had become expected guests. They were early this night because Meg had come to help Sandra prepare a plate of sliced smoked salmon, cream cheese, chopped onion and capers for the party.

"Nice to see you early," said Tom as he opened the door for the Looney's. "She's been thinking about that salmon plate all day."

"I've got it," said Meg, heading for the kitchen and leaving Ron to hang up her coat. "You guys go check on the ham."

"Not much to check," Tom said to her back. "I've got it all set."

"Not true, my friend," chimed Ron, heading for the table. "It needs a taste test before it can be declared ready for your guests."

"And you are just the one for that, aren't you?"

"Hey, I thought this was my role at this 'professional' party. I'm the only other Razorback here with the experience to judge how well the ham is prepared."

"You know that everyone else here has eaten Arkansas ham for the last five years and they all consider themselves now to be experts."

"And you know the difference between five years at once a year and a lifetime being raised on this stuff." Ron carefully tweezed off some meat from the bottom, layered it on a biscuit with horseradish sauce and grinned at Tom. "This is just like being home."

"Good to hear, because after the guests leave, all those who 'felt at home' need to stay and help with the clean up."

Ron said something that sounded remotely like "Happy to do so," but it was difficult to understand him with his mouth full.

As the guests arrived, usually bringing a bottle of wine or a box of candies as a gift to the host, the conversation increased around the dining room table. Everyone wanted to start there and did not move on until they had an ample supply of ham and bread. Then side conversations began to pick up around the scattered food settings throughout the house.

Tom was a busy man for the first half hour, hanging up coats, taking drink orders and placing gifts on the staircase in the front hall. There were guests with whom he had not spoken since last year's party and they made promises to catch up, but only after a visit to the dining room table. The wife of the Chief of Pulmonary brought baked raspberry Brie that required Sandra to find an appropriate place for it on the top of the piano.

Within the next hour all invitees had arrived, sampled the ham and drifted into conversations with others throughout the house. Vacation photos were shared. Experiences with different age school children became a major topic with problems and solutions floating around the rooms. And so it went until the first couple said their goodbyes. Then the parade for coats and hugs at the door began in earnest. Within 20 minutes the Bollings and the Looneys were left with the cleanup task.

Later, after all the dishes were safely returned to the kitchen and the women were carefully wrapping remaining food for storage, Tom and Ron sat in the living room to stay out of the way.

"Beer?" Tom asked.

"I think the answer has something to do with the Pope and going in the woods," nodded Ron. Tom made the treacherous trip into the kitchen for the drinks and back out without imperiling the work being done there.

They clinked the bottles and drank deeply.

""I'm guessing you don't put this out for the guests because you don't want them drinking and driving," Ron observed waving his longnecker.

"Responsible pub owner, that's me," Tom replied. "You have any funny cases I haven't heard about?"

"Well, I don't think I told you about the guy that tried to hold up a bakery with a knife."

"How'd that go?"

"Poorly right from the start. All the employees are behind those big glass cases and while the guy is yelling at one of them to open the cash register, another one just picks up the phone and calls it in. Squad cars are outside the store in three minutes and the perp tries to run. Didn't get to the corner."

"Drugged up?"

"Like a kite in March wind. It was actually easier than catching the guy who killed his dead wife with a shotgun."

"I don't know that story," Tom said.

Ron explained the call one Saturday morning to the Grant residence and how Grant had set up his neighbor to be a witness that would absolve him of the murder but the guy remembered Grant was wearing a sweatshirt and that led to realizing his duplicity and then to a confession before leaving the premises.

"You really have a lot of things to talk to Meg about after work, don't you?" Tom asked.

"Oh yeah. There's some belief that cops shouldn't talk about those things with civilians. But if I didn't talk to her I'd probably burn out. You know how wives can sometimes put just the right words on a subject and everything seems so much clearer?"

"Sure I do. Sandra and I have talked about things since med school. The kids call her 'the other doctor Bolling' because of her understanding of medical issues. And she has walked me through some inter-personal issues that I could easily have blown all out of proportion."

"They sure know what to say - and when to say it." They nodded to each other. "Anything important going on at your house?"

Tom told Ron about the discovery of attempted murder by one of the residents and all about the arsenic and the wife's revenge and how they worked with the county police.

"That's really good, Tom. I hadn't heard that story. All in the fingernails, huh? I bet that resident is the hero of New City, right?"

"Yes he was. For a few months but now he's seeing attempted murder everywhere."

"What do you mean, everywhere?"

"Well he's got a bee in his shorts about this one guy, we don't even know his name. Some homeless guy. But Ben is convinced somebody is trying to kill him."

"Why?"

"I don't know why. I don't recall that Ben came up with a motive.?

"I mean why does Ben think somebody's trying to kill this guy?"

" Ben found a bottle of high grade expensive whiskey on him when the guy was so drunk we had to dialyze him."

"That's all?"

"Well, no. He came to see me today because the guy showed up again. This time with a heroin overdose. And Ben is convinced the guy is not a druggie, because he has no track marks."

"And you don't think that's odd?"

"Maybe a little. But it doesn't make any sense for someone to be trying to 'off' some homeless guy," Tom said, a trifle defensively.

"Except he wasn't always homeless. Who knows who used to be."

"Not us for sure. We don't even have a name."

"What you do have is what sounds like two very unusual things happening to the same man." Ron had his chin down and was looking at Tom from under his eyebrows.

"What? Are you thinking Ben is right about these events being attempted murder?" Tom was surprised at Ron's reaction to the stories, but not as surprised as he was at Ron's next comment.

"I think you ought to cut the kid some slack," he said. "I think he may be right."

CHAPTER 27

Monday, January 6

Neither Tom nor Beverly had forgotten the issue regarding Nancy Hawes' Utilization Review material from a few months back. Tom especially felt that the whole issue around the review and the first presentation of it in the Morning Meeting was another example of the tension between him and the leaders of the Nursing Service. Early in his tenure as chief of staff Tom had lunch with Roslyn and she brought up her concern about nurses being 'handmaidens' to the doctors. Tom was unabashedly astounded and said so. He had never had such an opinion of nurses and was unaware of such behavior in the military.

His outspoken belief that such an attitude was not common clearly set a negative tone for his relationship with both Roslyn and Alena. From that point on they tended to bring 'concerns' of nursing service to the morning meeting in an effort to provide examples of outdated physician attitudes toward nurses. On at least two occasions Tom's response was impolite, to say the least and the battle lines had been drawn ever since.

So it was natural for Tom to look at the Utilization Review material and Nancy's data analysis as another skirmish in the Nurse v. Physician tournament. But Tom was a better administrator than that and accepted the truth of the nurse's analysis as a physician-educator's problem. He didn't stop there, however. He had learned over the years that there was more to a simple data analysis than usually was evident at first. Many times he had watched someone faced with data and analysis they didn't like responding by saying, "So, you've got your data, well, I've got mine." He knew from experience that such differences in opinion could only be solved by agreeing to work with the same data. When he shared this conviction with Beverly he found her to have very similar beliefs. Beverly was an intuitive administrator with years of experience in medical affairs and had a second sense about what she referred to as 'other people's data'. Anyone who knew Beverly's background was aware that she had a Master's degree in Public Health and assumed that her data handling capability came from that experience.

Certainly she had learned statistical analysis and data handling techniques as part of that degree. What others did not know was that she also had started a Masters in Business Administration degree several years before coming to New City. Beverly did not finish that degree because of personal issues and subsequent financial shortages. But she learned several things from her short time in the business program. She read Peter Drucker, guru to the business community, and learned from him a lesson she applied over and over in her later career.

Drucker said, at one time, "The greatest problem with American business is the intense interest in getting the right answer, when we should be more concerned with asking the right question." Beverly had come to understand that 'other people's data' had almost always been collected to 'get an answer' and she was not at all certain that the data collectors were ever asking the right question. Her insistence on bringing this perspective into every conversation about medical data in the aggregate was something Tom had learned to appreciate and to foster.

Tom and Beverly usually had time for a quiet chat about things in general several times a week. Tom insisted they take time away from the hurly-burly of the immediate to think about larger issues and the future rather than always spending their time intensely focused on that day's problem. And they each had expressed more than once their individual concern about the Utilization Review data. Beverly had suggested to Tom how she had wondered what question Nancy had been answering. Together they discussed whether there was a better question. Beverly had worried and thought and cogitated on this issue for several weeks and discussed a possibility with Tom. With his approval she had asked Andy McCall to come to her office for a consult.

Andy had come to Beverly's office right away. He was a boyish 30-something that dressed like he forgot he was going to be in public, shirt of many colors, barely tucked in, ragged jeans, and penny loafers without socks. Behind all that glitz, however, was a computer whiz and a crack data analyst. He worked in the hospital IT department as the chief programmer and analyst and had several regularly assigned tasks of data aggregation and analysis. His assignments were always at the behest of Sam Mastone. Sam wanted to have the data analytics he desired in a timely fashion and had resisted allowing the IT office to spend time collecting data or pumping out analytics for the clinical faculty fearing that would slow down response to his own questions. But what Andy really loved was diving in to the hospital data to get answers to new questions and that's what he had hoped Beverly was expecting for him to do.

The two of them spent a couple of hours a week puzzling through the various possible questions that would have relevant information for Tom and that Beverly thought could help keep Sam Mastone from meddling in clinical issues. They discussed several potential measures and ultimately agreed that they were thinking too narrowly. One afternoon in early December, they had come to agreement that they were really looking for some 'leading indicators' rather than what Nancy had been doing, finding a problem that already existed.

Beverly thought that the New City data programs were sufficiently honed in on the inpatient population since they already knew day-to-day numbers and had trending data on average length of stay, bed occupancy and certain Occurrence Screens like readmissions and returns to the OR. She pushed Andy to turn their analysis to focus on outpatient care and asked him to run a few data pulls for simple questions of outpatient clinic activity. They discussed whether this activity would affect his work for Sam; assured that it would not Beverly pressed him get it done.

A little over a week later Andy brought some very interesting information to their regular meeting. His data pulls indicated that, contrary to what had happened in year's past, the number of new patients was decreasing for the hospital as a whole. Andy was able to track patients new to the system by their social security number; he already did a routine analysis for Sam looking at the mix of payers they were caring for each quarter. New City had made its initial entry into the Cincinnati medical scene by being willing to take Medicare patients in the first few years after the program began. As the hospital grew and developed a reputation, particularly with its affiliation with the medical school, more privately insured patients began to seek care at New City.

Every quarter, Andy produced a report for the hospital director showing the current and trending levels of payer mix over Medicare, Medicaid and the remaining category, 'Other', which included private insurance, self-insured or other forms of payment. This report had always been framed in the form of a pie chart and represented the proportion of total hospital income drawn from each of these sources. What was not shown, because Sam never asked for it, was the total number of patients seen and treated in that quarter. Andy had pulled that number and recognized that, for several months, the number of new patients seen had been slowly drifting downward.

He and Beverly poured over this data for an hour, asking each other several questions trying to understand the importance of the analysis. Finally, Beverly asked, 'If we are enrolling fewer patients, are we also treating fewer patients?" That should also be reflected in the data and should be mirrored in the financial postings.

Andy already knew the answer to that and said, "We actually are seeing fewer cases but the number hasn't fallen outside the 10% variance Mr. Mastone set for warning."

Beverly chewed on this thought. She understood that Mastone realized that a fall outside of a 10% variance would indicate a problem, therefore data that indicated a trend toward that level of activity would be a 'leading indicator' like she wanted. But, as she also knew, both

Tom and Sam would immediately ask "Why?" So Beverly and Andy turned their attention to what the possible causes might be for the falling number of new patients.

They each thought of a few ideas and Andy took those ideas into data pulls and cross-analysis. The third big pull seemed to have some validity so Andy went back and pulled three full years of activity, did the display and analyzed the outcomes. He had been very excited to tell Beverly about his findings.

With a high degree of certainty, Andy's analysis of the data identified an almost inverse linear relationship between new patients enrolling in a given month and the increase in waiting time for a new patient appointment in certain specialty clinics at the hospital. A few years ago, the Urology clinic had been the major cause of a falloff in new enrollees. No one knew that at the time because no one asked Andy to look at the relevant data. When the Urology clinic waiting time dropped, however, the new enrollee numbers began to rise. But Andy could now show a recurrent steady drop in recruitment of new patients inversely related to the slowly increasing wait time for new patient appointments in General Medicine clinics.

Bev had found the 'leading indicator' she was seeking. She knew Tom would be pleased with their work even though he would also be annoyed that he had another outpatient clinic headache.

CHAPTER 28

Wednesday, January 15

Henry Dunstan, chief of General Medicine, respected researcher and well-published academician leaned comfortably back in the cushioned chair in Tom's office and asked, "What do you expect me to do, Tom? We're seeing patients that need to be seen and every one of the docs in those clinics is working 20-24 patients a day. I can feed them Wheaties if you want but it won't make them go any faster." He watched Tom take a deep breath but before he could speak, Dunstan went on, "I know you got some data. I have data, too. Shortly after you made those changes in Urology, our follow-up visits went up. Now that Cardiology is down a couple of slots, patients we would normally refer up to them have become ours to care for." Dunstan drew himself up to his full height, which was over six foot two inches and tall even sitting down. His half-glass spectacles sat low on his thin nose and he looked over them at Tom. Usually when he did that people on the receiving end felt they were downhill from a natural force. "That's why our waiting times are long. We are carrying the hospital on our backs."

Tom wasn't having any of the posturing, however. He said, as calmly as he could at the moment, "Henry, I don't know what your data shows but I'm certain it shows just what you said; that the doctors in General Medicine are working hard and filling their days with outpatient visits. I don't think you heard me clearly when I explained the data in this folder. It doesn't have anything to do with working hard. I believe you. I think the General Medicine faculty members are a vital part of our program and I know they carry an additional burden with their attending responsibilities. Don't think for a moment that I believe your people are slackers."

"Then what do you think is the way for us to see more people, Tom?"

"I didn't ask you to see more people. I said very plainly that you need to get your waiting time for new appointments shorter. They're now over three months. A couple of years ago they were 5-7 days."

"Dammit, Tom, all of us are working hard down there and the only way we can shorten the waiting time is to see more visits."

"You remember what Bobby Kennedy said about working hard?"

With a sigh, Henry slumped back in his chair, "No, Tom, I don't. I don't think I ever knew."

"Right after the Bay of Pigs fiasco, one of the reporters asked him what went wrong. Bobby shook his head and said, 'We don't really know. We thought we were doing great. We were working really hard.'"

"So you think General Medicine is like the Bay of Pigs?"

"I didn't say that and I don't think that. But maybe you're a little like Bobby Kennedy."

"In what way?"

"He thought that working hard was going to lead to success-and it didn't. It puzzled him because he didn't see another way to have done things."

"So now I'm narrow-minded?'

"Geez, Henry, can you get out of your ego for minute? Yes, I do think you have had some trouble seeing how to fix this problem because you only know one way-do more of what you are already doing and see more people. And for that to be a solution you think it will require more doctors and more clinics, right?" He noticed that Henry was nodding and went on, "It's just like the dialysis unit. No matter how many chairs you have or how many sessions you run a week, at some point the seats are all full and what do you do with the next patient? The guys who have run most of the dialysis programs answer the same way you do: get more seats. They open up a new clinic. That's not the best solution unless you always make money on the margin."

Tom paused for a beat. Henry was looking at him with less antagonism and at least a little interest. Tom continued, "You know what the best of the dialysis units did when they saw that crunch coming, Henry? They did something different. They turned to the patients and started a home dialysis training program. Once they figured out what was needed, they found they could train patients in a matter of a few weeks to carry out their dialysis treatment at home. And they found that patients could do the dialysis away from the hospital without highly professional oversight and yet do it safely, efficiently and, big bonus for the patients, at their convenience."

Another pause. "And do you know what the outcomes were? Lower overall cost per dialysis, happier and more compliant patients, and a lower mortality rate. And those weren't the goals that anyone was initially seeking. They just wanted to be able to provide care for the patients that needed them."

Henry sighed deeply and said, "I'm still short-sighted. I don't see a way to cut down on the waiting time without churning patients through our clinics faster."

"May I make a suggestion?" Tom asked.

"Of course. I thought that's why we were meeting."

"Have you thought about going to Same Day appointments?"

"Wait. You mean like the 'concierge doctors'?

"Not exactly. I had this problem with long waiting times in the Air Force at one posting. In the Air Force, of course, the patients really had no other option and I had to get it fixed. We did it by looking at the practice patterns and instituting 'same day' options."

"No offense, Tom, but you could order that in the military. We don't really work that way at New City."

"And I know that, Henry. I didn't order anything in the Air Force. Everyone agreed to try it."

"Yeah, well, that's not going to work here, I can tell you."

"How do you know that?"

"Because I work in that clinic every week. I see patients down there and I talk with the faculty and the students, that's how. And they are all busy running from pillar to post just trying to keep up. If you want them to be more productive, try putting some more help in the clinic."

"Maybe I can do that. Some PAs or NPs maybe."

"I meant more physicians," Dunstan said.

"Not likely right now," Tom said. Then switching thoughts he asked, "What's the usual reappointment time for hypertensive patients?"

"Uh, three or six months, I guess. Why?"

"How about diabetics?"

"Three months, and again, why?"

"What is the evidence for either of those practices?" Tom asked sitting back in his chair as if waiting for a lengthy explanation.

"Well, I'm not sure … " stalled Henry.

"Well, I am," Tom asserted. "There is none. Evidence I mean. There is common practice and 'how we have always done it', but there is not any medical evidence that we maintain better control of these patients' conditions or prevent hospitalizations or strokes or anything else by seeing the patients more frequently."

"We prevent those things with good control of their blood pressure and their blood sugar," Henry argued.

"That's true. So why don't you have them in the clinic for checkup every day? You'd have more information and a better chance of controlling things. Right?"

"C'mon, Tom. You know that's not practical."

"Of course I do. But just like those dialysis patients, I also know you can get them involved in their own care and likely cut down on the need to see them so often."

"What do you mean?"

" Every drug store sells blood pressure cuffs and all your diabetics have their blood sugar monitors, right?" When Henry nodded Tom went on, "So, teach them how to do their own blood pressure monitoring at home and tell them to come in for evaluation once a year or whenever the pressure is too high for too long. One of the PAs can teach them that. And for every hypertensive patient you move from four visits a year to one visit a year you have freed up three patient care slots!"

"You know that won't work, Tom."

"I know no such thing. Saw it happen in the Air Force."

"With a bunch of healthy young adults, sure."

"Henry, you're a smart man and should know better than that. Our medicine clinics in the Air Force were just like the ones here at New City. Young recruits were rare in those clinics; they were usually treated in the dispensary. Medicine clinics mostly saw 10-20 year veterans and their wives plus retirees. I've been in your clinics and your patients look just like the ones in the Air Force."

"I just don't think our doctors will go for that."

"I'm sure you're right," Tom smiled. "No one wants to work less hard."

"I mean they will be concerned about how well the patients can do unsupervised."

"You can point out that they are currently unsupervised for 89 out of 90 days. And the diabetics can have access to a clinic run by an NP if they have difficulty controlling their sugar. The nurse and a dietician do most of the work in that regard anyway, don't they? Your doctors just make a referral."

Henry nodded slowly and said, "Yes, I think so. That's what I do."

Tom sensed he was gaining ground and continued, "Look, why don't you see if a couple of your people would like to try this? They have a panel, right? With a little time you could see which patients they are following at 3-4 month intervals and see if they really need that. If not, I'll put a PA down there to help train the patients in self-care and teach them how to get a same day appointment if they need it. We can try this out for a few months."

"Yeah. Yes. I guess can do that."

"Really, Henry, I want this to come from you. I can take the blame if it doesn't work."

Henry thought this offer over for a few moments before taking a deep breath and agreeing, "Tell you what, I'll look at my panel first. It's a little smaller than the others and it'll be easier to go through." He was not completely convinced but was willing to take the first look and that was what Tom considered a 'win-win' at the moment.

"Would you like some help with that?"

"What do you mean?"

"I can ask Beverly and Andy to help with pulling some lists for you."

"Actually that would be good. I was sitting here worrying about how to get that data."

They shook hands and Henry left. Tom sat back in his chair and thought, "This persuasion business is definitely harder than command. And so much more satisfying."

CHAPTER 29

Saturday, February 2

Ben Nealy had finished his Saturday rounds and checked out to the resident on call. His day was free and he had no plans other than having to get to the cleaners and by the grocery store for some replenishment for his barren refrigerator. On call, and eating at the hospital every third day and grabbing fast food on most of the other days meant that he had allowed his 'in house' supplies to get a little bare. He was thinking about a grocery list as he left the ward and decided to drop down to the Emergency area to talk with Susan.

He found her in the back room and sat down across the little table from her and asked, "Do you really have to work today? We could go to the Observatory!"

"You know better than that. We can do the Observatory later."

"Like tonight?"

"Let's see, Ben. It could be a really bad day."

Just then they heard the scurrying activity and raised voices that meant a new patient had arrived. Susan scrambled to her feet and was out the door without saying goodbye. Ben sat there for a moment and decided he could get the groceries on his way back to his apartment and started out of the area, intending to use the main door since it was closer to the parking lot.

As he entered the main hallway he noticed a clamor of people around a figure still on the ambulance gurney and overheard the story being told to the emergency resident. The police had been scouting an area known for drugs and found this guy in an alley. He didn't respond to Narcan but he looked drugged and they called it in. The officers had waited with the man until the ambulance arrived. The Emergency Medical Technicians told the resident he was gasping 'like that' all the way to the hospital. Ben went over to see what 'like that' looked like and recognized the patient.

"Holy shit!" he exclaimed, taking immediate charge. "I know this guy. Get me a 'scope."

Nurses sprang into action turning the patient, placing a pillow under his shoulders and handing Ben the laryngoscope from a nearby room. Without bothering to take off his jacket, Ben dropped his briefcase on the floor and grabbed the laryngoscope and swiped his hand through the old man's mouth before he slid the metal blade into the patient's mouth. A nurse handed him an intubation tube and Ben easily slid it into the patient as someone came forward with an Ambu bag that he quickly attached to the tube. The emergency resident put his stethoscope on the patient's chest and Ben pushed on the Ambu. "It's in," said the resident and everyone took a deep breath. The entire procedure took less than a minute. Ben relinquished the Ambu to one of the nurses and turned to the resident.

"I know this guy. His name is 'Barry' and he left here AMA a couple of weeks ago. Let's get him up to the ICU. I'll take him on my service." The uniformed police were already heading out the door and the EMTs quickly and efficiently moved 'Barry' to an ED bed and hustled their gurney out the door.

One of the nurses had called the ICU and was signaling to Ben. She handed him the phone.

"This is Doctor Nealy."

"This is Cinda. What's this about a patient coming up?"

"He just rolled into the ED with some kind of respiratory arrest. We've got a tube in him and we're bagging him right now but I'll need a vent when he gets to the Unit."

"We've got a bed. I'll get Respiratory to bring us a ventilator."

"Thanks, Cinda. We'll be right up."

Ben smiled at the nurse handling the Ambu bag and said, "Want to take a little trip?"

She smiled back and nodded. He summoned one of the aides to help with moving the bed and they started down the hall toward the elevators.

A short time later 'Barry' was propped up in an ICU bed, attached to a ventilator and breathing a regular 16 times a minute with occasional sighs. Ben was in the Unit, and had overseen the placement of a central intravenous line in the right subclavian vein. He sat at the Nurses' station and looked at the initial blood work finding nothing to explain the collapse he had witnessed in the ED. He ordered a blood tube be sent to the lab for a toxicology screen along with a urine sample.

He watched 'Barry' as he lay quietly in that lonely bed. Apparently the struggling Ben had seen in the ED was 'Barry' fighting to breathe. Ben remembered it was a scary sight, the twitching respirations that were rapid and shallow as well as totally ineffective. Ben didn't get a blood gas sample until 'Barry' had arrived in the ICU and had been helped with his breathing for at least 15 minutes. Those blood gases looked fairly good except for the profound acidosis. Ben knew that meant that 'Barry' had been breathing ineffectively for many minutes before he got to the ED. How long was not certain but brain damage was now the major question.

After an acute event that deprived the brain of oxygen for more than three or four minutes the likelihood of anoxic brain damage was high and increased the longer the time of deprivation. The first twenty-four hours after the insult were the most important in predicting recovery; any serious lack of brain activity after that held very small chance of recovery. Ben watched as 'Barry' remained unmoving in the bed and felt the opportunity for ever getting to the bottom of the mystery surrounding this old man slipping away.

The charge nurse in the ICU came over to Ben and said, "Look. We got this. He hasn't changed since you got him in here and you're just getting in our way. Why don't you just go home? We'll take good care of him."

"I know that, Cinda. I just want to be here if he wakes up."

"You know that's not likely. Go home."

"Yeah, OK," Ben replied dispiritedly. He grabbed his briefcase and left.

CHAPTER 30

Sunday, February 3

The following morning Ben came by the ICU on his way to the ward. He checked the nurses' notes on 'Barry' from the night shift. They had noted no spontaneous movement but he had been successfully weaned off the respirator and was breathing well on his own. Ben stood at the foot of the bed and looked at the frail old body lying still and quiet except for his respirations.

"What was the deal, buddy?" he asked of the man in the bed. "Who are you running from?" As always, 'Barry' had no useful response.

The head nurse in the ICU was Eddie Bostick, a forty-something stocky guy with a naturally bald head. He came up to Ben as he stood in the room and said, "Good morning, Dr. Nealy."

"Good morning, Eddie."

"You have a bed for him on the ward?"

"What? Oh, yeah. I don't know. I'm on way up there now."

"He doesn't need Intensive Care any more."

"Right. Yes. I can see that. I'll go find a bed for transfer."

"Thank you, doctor."

Later Ben wondered why Eddie, with whom he was usually on a first name basis, had acted so formal about the transfer request. He would ask Eddie about that the next time he saw him in the cafeteria.

Work rounds with the interns went smoothly and Ben found three empty beds on the ward. He asked his head nurse to arrange the transfer for 'Barry' and to put him somewhere near the nursing station. The nurse said those beds were usually for patients that needed close attention and there was another patient they were moving into the room closest to station. They looked at each other for several seconds before Ben saw the wisdom of the plan as the nurses saw things. He nodded and the head nurse dipped her head toward him and returned to making the bed transfer plans.

Ben went to the physician workroom and checked with Denis and Allison. They were engrossed in following through on items that came up on the rounds earlier; they indicated that they were able to handle their work and no longer needed his oversight. Ordinarily, having his interns show that degree of self-sufficiency would have made Ben feel pleased and satisfied. This time, however, he had a sinking feeling in his stomach that just like the interns no longer needed his guidance and assistance, 'Barry' was also beyond anything Ben could do to help him.

Ben walked to the library and studied the covers of the most recent journals and realized he had already seen them. He left and wandered up to the call area where the hospital had provided a break room for the trainees. It wasn't fancy but it did have a small refrigerator kept stocked with bottles of water and cans of soda, a small cabinet-top microwave, a mid-sized color television and two couches plus three overstuffed chairs. This is where the house staff congregated to watch March Madness or weekend football games. At least, the unmarried ones did. Ben found one other resident in the lounge area and they talked briefly of things in general but neither had much interest in talking so the conversation died into tolerant silence.

That lasted about ten minutes and then the other resident got up, waved and left. Ben stretched out on the couch and tried, for the third time, to make sense of the unknowns surrounding 'Barry'. He tried to do it without actually thinking about the dire circumstance of 'Barry's' condition.

Ben knew from first hand experience that 'Barry' lived on the street, homeless, dirty and poorly nourished for at least several months. Had he been there longer? How long? What was his circumstance that left him out on the street? Did he have family? Probably not or they would be helping him. Unless he was a 'black sheep' and had been rejected by the family. Was that why he kept his name a secret? Was he embarrassed over some past failure?

Was it possible that 'Barry' had been in Witness Protection? If so, could he have become so addicted to alcohol that he was abandoned by the Marshals? Maybe he couldn't remember either his real name or the name he was hiding under.

That did not agree with the innate intelligence Ben could see at times in 'Barry's' eyes. Or did some other feeling fool him?

Ben lay there on the couch and drifted into a shallow sleep that lasted an hour or so. The two residents on call that day came into the area making considerable noise arguing about which room they would claim for sleeping quarters. Ben sat up and looked at his watch. He remembered that he had never made the grocery run he had intended when 'Barry' was admitted. He decided he had better get that done before the sun went down; he and the team were on call the next day and he knew he needed some sleep.

CHAPTER 31

Monday, February 4

The next morning brought no significant change. 'Barry' had been relocated to the ward from the ICU and was perfectly stable. The ward nurses were unhappy about having a total care patient on the ward since they were not staffed with the male nurses' aides common to long term care areas who helped with the issues of turning and transfers of such patients. Ben listened to these comments during his early rounds with the head nurse and promised that he would start work on placement for 'Barry' in some long-term care facility right away.

Ben's new attending was one of the pulmonary faculty who had finished training just three years before. He was bright, savvy and not interested in dragging out the experience of attending rounds. After seeing all the other patients, Ben dismissed the interns and made a three-minute presentation of 'Barry's' case to the attending and asked specifically what he should have been looking for that would cause the respiratory paralysis that now seemed to have disappeared.

The pulmonologist was helpful with a modest list of causes but none of them fit the scenario Ben had witnessed. This wasn't shock or blocked airway, didn't act like a pulmonary embolus, it looked like muscle dysfunction. And what mostly puzzled Ben was the fact that the problem appears to have vanished..

"Guillain-Barre?" suggested the attending.

"Does that go away, like this?" probed Ben.

"No. And neither does myasthenia. So I'm stumped. Let me know what you find out," he commented as he left the ward. Ben had heard that request several times in his last year of training. He found that when he couldn't quickly discern cause and diagnosis in a difficult case that his request for help from specific specialists frequently was, "Let me know what you find out."

Initially Ben had thought he was being dismissed by the more senior faculty but lately had come to realize that his own level of insight and expertise was fairly close to theirs and when he didn't figure out the puzzle, they were not likely to, either. Further, he now realized that they truly wanted to learn what the answer was and they trusted that he would find it.

Ben watched his attending walk toward the elevators and saw Dr. Song get off the elevator and start toward the ward.

"I wonder what she's doing up here?" Ben thought. He went into the doctor's workroom, sat down and rubbed his face. He had about thirty minutes before he was going to meet Susan for lunch and he thought he would just hit the internet for some help.

Behind him he heard, "Dr. Nealy?"

Dr. Song was standing in the doorway holding a folder and indicating she would like his attention.

"Yes, Dr. Song. Please sit down," he said indicating any of the several empty chairs in the room.

"I have some very interesting results for you," she said.

Ben's mind spun around for few seconds wondering when he had asked for help from Dr. Song. Then he remembered she was also the toxicologist in the hospital. "Is this about 'Barry'?

"Or whoever he is. Yes, it is."

"I hope it explains what went on."

"I think so. But first, are you aware that a request for an examination by a pathologist is the same as a consult?"

"Uh, well, yes, I guess so."

"Your request for a toxicology screen was really a consult sent to me."

"I guess I didn't know that," Barry replied.

"We can set up the lab and run a chemical analysis on blood and urine for every toxin or poison known to man but that would take days and lots more money than we have," Song explained in a straight-forward manner.

"Oh," said Ben, getting the feeling he was not only going to get a lecture on resource management but also was about to be told his request was useless.

"But I always see these kind of requests as a consult. Instead of having the technicians blindly do every test they could imagine, I went to see your patient to decide what kind of toxins we should be looking for."

"Great!" Ben said, his spirits rising.

"Your note indicated he was having trouble breathing when you first saw him, is that right?"

"Yes. His respirations were shallow and ragged."

"And there was nothing in his mouth?"

"No. I checked and the 'scope showed nothing."

"Once you got the tube in place, was it hard to bag him?"

"I don't think so. I only did it for a minute before one of the nurses took over."

"But it wasn't like he had stiff lungs?"

"No. He's kinda small and it seemed easy."

"Do you know how long was he on the ventilator?" Dr. Song was leaning forward now.

"Several hours I'd guess. I stayed in the ICU for a couple of hours after I tubed him but then the nurses kicked me out. They extubated him sometime later."

"They were able to extubate him about an hour after you left. So in less than four hours he completely recovered his ability to breathe on his own." Monique said this with the attitude that it should explain everything. Ben sat looking at her, obviously expecting more.

"It had to be a short-term paralytic," she explained.

"What?"

"A short-term paralytic," she said again, a little more slowly.

"Some kind of poison?"

"Oh yes. Definitely. And I know exactly what kind. And I know that only because you were smart enough to get a tox screen."

Ben completely skipped past the praise and said, "You know what happened?"

"As I said," Monique repeated, "I most definitely do. It was Sux and I'm sure of it."

"What sucks?" Ben asked with eyebrows furrowing.

"Sux. It's short for succinylcholine."

"Curare?"

"Well, it's like the active ingredient in curare, yes. Studies show that it is metabolized fairly quickly and is gone from the blood in 10-15 minutes."

The timing Dr. Song was suggesting puzzled Ben. "He was down 10-15 minutes before he even got here. And I didn't think to get a tox tube until after we got him into ICU. That's way more than an hour. How'd you find it then?"

"Because it breaks down into a byproduct that hangs around for hours in the blood and is in the urine for days. Something called succinylmonocholine or SMC. And your boy was loaded with it. So, I'm positive he was hit with Sux and would have died a respiratory death if you hadn't got that tube in him and got him on a respirator."

This time Ben took the compliment. He smiled and said, "Thanks for the consult, Dr. Song," as he winked at her.

CHAPTER 32

Wednesday, February 5

Two days later 'Barry' had not recovered. He was breathing on his own but had not moved since arrival in the ICU. Now he lay in the back hall on the ward where Ben visited twice a day, still hoping for some sign of recovery.

Ben had presented his 'attempted murder' case to the attending who was sympathetic after hearing about the succinylcholine but wasn't sure what else to do. Ben had taken his case back to the chairman. Dr. Abert was also more supportive, especially after he performed his own examination of 'Barry' and came away convinced that he was not an intravenous drug user.

Abert and Ben met with Tom again and convinced him that 'Barry's' case should be a serious contender for 'attempted murder'. Tom had visited the ward twice to check on his progress and, consequently began to raise the question of ongoing care for the man.

Tom's first thought was that 'Barry' no longer needed treatment in an acute care setting and spoke directly to Ben about arranging for his transfer to a long term care facility. Ben had already talked at length with a social worker about the concept and she had explained to Tom that she could not find a facility willing to take a non-insured patient like this.

Tom also raised the issue of resuscitation orders for 'Barry'. He and Ben agreed that the current situation did not suggest a likelihood of recovery but Ben wanted a better measure of that. He had requested a Neurology consult regarding potential recovery.

The neurology workup was not encouraging. The Neurology Fellow, Aram Nabizedeh, sat down with Ben to explain. "You know his Glasgow Coma Score is as low as it could be, right?"

"Sure, and it hasn't changed."

"Well, I read the chart and we both agree that cerebral hypoxia is the most likely cause here."

"That's what I think, yes," Ben replied.

"I did a complete exam as you requested," Aram said. "I understand you have some history with this fellow."

"History, yes. Attachment, not really. I just think somebody has been trying to kill this man for months."

"Well, if that's true, I think they have succeeded."

"Explain."

"As you are aware he has decerebrate posturing and no spontaneous movement. He does not respond to pain and he has no eye movement. Corneal reflex is absent and pupillary response is slow. And he is afebrile and has no meningismus."

"You mean this isn't like meningitis or an infection."

"Exactly. I believe I can tell you his dismal prognosis from just this examination but for you, my friend, I will get an EEG before I make the final decision."

"Thanks, Ram. I didn't really expect anything good. I just wanted to be sure before we make him DNR."

"Actually I think Do Not Resuscitate is completely appropriate from my examination."

"I know. But as soon as he is DNR, the chairman and the chief of staff are gonna make me place him in some nursing home."

"And that would be bad, because …?"

"Not bad really. Just because nobody is going to take the attempted murder seriously after he is transferred."

"Do you ever get tired of carrying the world on your shoulders, Ben?"

Ben looked at Aram, "Don't know what you mean, Ram. Let's get on with the EEG. I gotta talk to somebody else about a new idea."

Two hours later with the EEG completed, Aram and Ben met again.

"Just like I thought, the tracings are essentially flat. This is a dead cortex."

"No chance of improvement over time?"

"If I was seeing this tracing right at the beginning I would doubt recovery. Changes can happen but this is now far enough away from the insult that I'm sure he will never recover."

"So he's just going to lay like that until he gets an infection and dies?"

"You know how that goes. I'm sorry. Is there anything else I can do to help you?"

"No. Thanks, Ram. I'll take it from here."

Ben spent a few minutes planning out his next steps and then went to find the chairman. In Abert's office he reported the neurology findings and they both agreed that they were not unexpected. Ben then explained what he wanted to talk to the chief of staff about.

Tom asked the two of them to meet in his office and he asked Beverly to sit in. The chairman took the upholstered chair and Ben sat in the straight back chair next to the desk of the chief of staff. Beverly brought an extra chair in from her office and sat next to Ben.

"Sir, we have completed neurological testing on 'Barry' and the outcome is pretty much what we all expected. He is essentially brain dead. Got some brain-stem functions but no cortex and virtually no chance of functional recovery."

"All that is simply confirmatory, it doesn't change what we need to do. You know that, don't you Ben?"

"Well, yes sir. Certainly if you mean changing our attitude about his recovery."

"That's not all. He is officially no longer in need of acute care in the hospital. He should be moved to some long term care facility."

"I think we all agree on that, sir. But our social worker, Alice Hampton, cannot find one that will accept him. No insurance and no family."

"Why can't we find a family?"

"He has never had identification. We don't really even know his name. In fact, I was hoping that you could help us out there, sir."

Tom looked steadily at Ben as he said, "In what way?"

"Well, sir, you have a friend in the Cincinnati Police Department. Maybe he could help us get an identity. It's possible that 'Barry' has a record of some kind and he could help us identify him from that and then we could find the family.

Tom sat quietly for a minute and then looked at Beverly who shrugged her shoulders.

"That's actually not a bad idea, Ben," Tom said as he stole a glance at the chairman who was smiling and nodding. "My friend in the police department just might be the very answer." Tom did not tell anyone that barely a month ago Ron had said that Ben was probably right about the attempts on 'Barry's' life. He intended to keep that little piece of information between the two of them.

CHAPTER 33

Thursday, February 6

Tom called Ron later that day. "I got a favor to ask," he said in greeting.

"I'm not about to bring back that piece of pie I took home from the party."

"Well then, I'll see to it that you never get another."

"That's just mean. What do you need?"

"Remember me telling you about the case where one of our residents thought there was an attempt on a patient's life?"

"I remember an attempted murder scenario. Are you telling me it's happened again? At New City?"

"In a way. The guy is back as a patient and this time I am convinced someone tried to kill him. And they may have succeeded."

"What's that? You don't know? Can't you tell if he's dead or not?"

"It's a sticky situation in several regards, Ron. I need your help in identifying the guy. I think I told you that he is homeless, and that means he is also without insurance. Or any other way to pay for hospital care. We carry a small amount of bono work here but Mastone is watching that like a hawk. I've explained to you before that most of our patients are fully insured or they have Medicare so we get reimbursed for their care. But we don't get anything for caring for the uninsured unless they can pay out of their own pocket."

"Aren't you getting a little wound up in the for-profit aspect here?"

"Certainly more than usual and more than I'm comfortable with. Like I said we do some bono work all year long but this one case could use up all our planned effort in that regard."

"Why's that?"

"Because he is now total care."

"What's that mean to us guys in the Division?"

"He's in a brain dead coma. Doesn't do anything but breathe. We have to turn him every so often to keep him from getting bedsores. And nurses have to suction his secretions so he doesn't drown. That's what total care means."

"So why can't you send him to a nursing home?"

"They won't take him because he's uninsured. If we could track down his family perhaps they could help with his care. And we also need their input on decisions like resuscitation."

"And he has no name?"

"Made up name. No identification. Without that information we can't find the family."

"Oh, I see. He can't tell you anything?"

"That's what comatose means," Tom observed tensely.

"And this happened because. . .?"

"Apparently from another attempt."

"This sounds like you need more than help in identifying him." Ron sounded pleased at having gotten this information

"What do you mean?"

"I mean you need help in finding a murderer."

"That's not my job."

"Well, it'll be mine if you can convince me something's going on here."

"Bring a fingerprint kit and come see us," Tom said. "And we'll talk."

*   *   *

Ninety minutes later Tom and Ron walked on the ward. Tom had explained he and a 'friend' were going to examine 'Barry' and the nurses nodded to them as they passed.

"This is the same back hall, isn't it?" Ron said as they approached the room.

"Same hall, different floor," Tom answered briefly, not wanting to dwell on the subject of Ron's question.

At the bedside, Ron took out his fingerprint kit and picked up 'Barry's' stiff and resisting hand to clean the fingertips for printing.

"What the hell?" he muttered, looking at the upturned palm.

"What's the matter?" Tom asked.

"Look at this, my man," came the reply as Ron showed the palmar surface to Tom.

"What am I looking at?"

"No fingerprints!"

"What?" Tom exclaimed moving around the bed to get closer.

Ron was right, close examination of 'Barry's' fingers showed no evidence of the usual ridges; the tips were dirty but smooth. "This won't do us any good," Ron said. "Is this part of the medical condition?

"I don't think so," Tom said. "I'm not aware of anything causing this except some disease that makes the skin fall off. Which he doesn't have."

"You know, some big time criminals used acid or a knife to get rid of their finger prints," Ron said still fascinated by the absence. "But his fingers are just smooth, no scars or anything like that."

"Who does something like that?"

"Dillinger, for one. He had surgery and also tried using acid but the prints came back. Another guy got skin grafts from his chest."

"Have to be a big time criminal."

"Or really crazy. Except for the skin graft case, all the things people have tried were failures. The prints ultimately grew back out."

"So, now what do we do to find out who this guy really is?" Tom asked.

Ron silently shook his head before saying, "Damned if I know. I need to go talk with some folks."

CHAPTER 34

Thursday, February 6

Ben was musing to Susan during lunch about the mystery of 'Barry's' missing fingerprints.

"I think I know what's going on," he said taking a large bite of pizza.

"Really? I'd like to hear. And so would everybody else."

"Mmmph," he mumbled, then took a swig of his iced tea. "Caught me with my mouth full. Here's the way I put this together. 'Barry' is in the Witness Protection program. He was part of some gang activity somewhere like maybe Detroit and turned against the mob. Probably a hit man or something like that and they had his fingerprints removed to protect him. Then he got old and afraid the mob was going to have him killed so he turned on them and gave some information to the FBI. The gang got busted but 'Barry' had to run and somehow they found him."

"Well, that's pretty original," Susan said.

"Thank you," Ben said as he took another large bite of his pizza.

"I think your storyline has some holes," Susan stated with a grin , taking another bite of her lunch.

"Howz zat?"

"Well, I don't think the Witness Protection program puts their witness people into a homeless program, for one."

"Well, hmm. . . Maybe he escaped."

"Escaped from protection. To go hide on the streets of Cincinnati. Oh yeah, that's a very solid theory, my mistake," she smiled and he shook his head and asked, "Anything else?"

Susan went on, "I heard Dr. Abert and Dr. Anderson, the dermatologist, talking about the fingerprints and Anderson said it looked like chemicals or something and that they would grow back in a few months. How does that fit in your theory?"

"We don't have a few months to wait," Ben said, puzzled at her question. "You know he's not going to live long like this."

"I mean, how long have we known 'Barry'? Four or five months, right? If the mob removed his finger prints and then he worked for them and then he turned informant and then he got into Witness Protection and then they started chasing him … "

"Oh, yeah. I see. I still like the mob and the Witness Protection idea."

"Even if that has nothing to do with his fingerprints?"

"Yeah, I think so."

"My advice is stick to your day job. You're a good doctor and an average detective."

"We'll see," Ben retorted as he finished his pizza.

*   *   *

Ron was sitting in Tom's office using the upholstered 'dignitary' chair. They each had a cup of coffee from the Green Bean and Ron was probing Tom about the conversation he had just witnessed with Tom's favorite barista at the kiosk, Nick.

"So, Nick and you were together at Sig?" he asked, referring to references they had made about the area around Sigonella Air Base in Sicily.

"Not together, but only a few years apart. Didn't even know Nick until he started working here," Tom said. He leaned back in his chair. "I wasn't stationed there for a full tour. Had short tour there when I thought I was on the way to the sandbox."

"You didn't go to Iraq, did you?"

"No. Stuff heated up and I was diverted to Bagram. First time I met Nick he wanted to know where all I had been posted. And Sig was the only place we both knew. That's how he and I know about the black sand at Catonia."

"And all those little eating places in Taormina?" Ron asked as he sipped his coffee.

"Oh yeah. Couple of little holes in the wall right off the April 9 Piazza. Great food, and wonderful wine. One of the best postings ever."

"I felt that way about Germany. Bavaria in particular. And the beer."

"Good old days when you weren't chasing murderers, huh?"

"Speaking of which, I had an some ideas about this guy of yours. What's his name?"

"They call him 'Barry' for some reason," Tom replied.

"Well, if he's military we might could get a dental match from the military records."

"Nice thought but this guy is edentulous," Tom smiled wryly.

"Enough with the doctor talk. Can I get pictures of his teeth or not?"

"Actually, no. He has no teeth. Dentures but no native teeth."

Ron sat back in the chair and took a draw on his coffee. "Fortunately, that wasn't my best shot."

"What else you got, big boy?" Tom grinned at him.

"You're gonna like this one, warfighter," Ben said, setting his coffee down and leaning forward. "You know about the AFDIL?"

"I think so."

"The Armed Forces DNA Identification Laboratory at Dover."

"Yeah, I remember. We used that to identify remains."

"Right. So, I'm thinking if old 'Barry' was in service-anywhere-we can get a DNA match from the laboratory."

"If he was in the military."

"I looked them up on the way over here and I'll give them a call right away."

"Thanks, Ron. You really are good at your job," Tom said as he saluted Ron with his cup.

CHAPTER 35

Thursday, February 13

Tom was rummaging through some paperwork on his desk, checking the work of the credentialing and privileging committee before signing off on the new anesthesiologist. He appeared very intent on his review of the package but his mind wandered significantly from the folder. He wondered what had happened to Ron's contact with the DNA laboratory. He had taken the swab a week ago, but 'Barry' was still up there on the ward and now had some early signs of bed sores. He really needed to get into a long-term care facility.

"Dr. Bolling?" It was Mary Brighthouse, leaning in the doorway.

"Yes?"

"Dr. Dunstan is here to see you."

"Alright," Tom said. "Show him in."

The chief of General Medicine walked in smiling. "Tom."

"Henry, I got your note but I'd like a little more information than 'It's OK'. Have a seat. Can you enlighten me?

"Sure. Your idea seems to be working." Dunstan commented cheerily. "I thought you should know." He sat in the dignitary chair and comfortably crossed his legs.

"Tell me more. I always like to be right about something." Tom smiled and leaned back in his chair.

"Well, I presented your idea to the faculty. You probably recall that I wasn't enthused about the whole idea. But after Beverly and Andy brought me the data you promised, it did honestly look like my own clinic could get involved without a lot of concern about safety. So I made your pitch at the staff meeting and some of the younger ones said they'd like to try that."

Tom nudged him a little, saying, "And by 'that' you mean …?"

"The Same Day clinic idea. To be fair, I told them about my own hesitation and then discussed the data from my clinic. Looks like about half of my patients with hypertension, type 2 diabetes and asthma are very stable and I make almost no changes in their regimen when they come to clinic. I know these people very well and most of them are capable of a high degree of self-care. So, when I talked with the clinic physicians about the idea they were less skeptical than I anticipated. The ones most interested were some of the new faculty. Their clinics aren't so big yet and they thought they could get something going fairly quickly."

"And did they?"

"Oh, yes. One of them even said he had been thinking of doing this himself."

"It's always better when it's their idea."

"So three of them immediately started looking at their panel and talking to patients and even doing their own patient education. Now they're coming by my office at the end of the day almost every day this last week to say how well it's going."

"Really? That was only a month ago. What's going on that they're impressed with this so soon?"

"According to them, the patients are solidly in favor. They've heard stories about how hard it was to manage their appointments off in the future; something often came up and they couldn't reschedule because the book was so tight."

"How did you set it up?"

"Pretty much like you said," Henry replied as he shifted in the 'dignitary' chair and extended his legs. "They agreed on some basic rules like who should not be put on this schedule and worked with the clinic PA to arrange some teaching for patients and then they started talking to the patients. And many of them said 'yes'-after concern that they wouldn't be able to get an appointment if they needed one."

"How did you deal with that?" Tom asked

"The doctors told the patients if they couldn't get an appointment to call them directly. Gave them their office phone number. Patients were tickled."

"Huh," said Tom. "We didn't do that in the Air Force. Might've helped to speed things along."

"Well, it's been in play now for about three weeks. Not long enough to give it a real test or to see where the wheels are gonna fall off, but so far it's OK."

"How do you measure 'OK', Henry?"

"Right. You want some numbers."

"Facts."

"Facts, then. These three doctors are telling me they have open slots, just one or two, every day now and they are finished seeing patients and have their paperwork done before 5:00 o'clock."

"That's does sound like movement in the right direction. I'm pleased."

" I thought you would be. I'm surprised, frankly but I'm glad it seems to be working. I'm not seeing that big a change in my schedule as of yet but I have a larger panel and longer wait time than any of the three involved in this change."

"What about the rest of the faculty? Are they impressed?" Tom asked.

"Well, yes and no. But that's another interesting thing. A couple of the older ones have said they want to try pushing same day in their clinic. They actually don't look like they're worried about the younger ones teaching them something."

"You mean they are acting like adults."

"Perhaps, but the really fascinating thing to me is the way the skeptics have actually bonded with the same day practitioners for research."

"What's that about?" Tom leaned forward to get the full perspective on this totally unanticipated development.

"Well, the skeptics are worried that not seeing patients regularly will lead to increased hospitalizations that could have been prevented. So they challenged the Same Day clinics to collect data on their patients' long-term outcomes. They are getting together after clinic on Thursdays to plan out a clinical research project. Matched controls from the skeptics clinics against ones from the 'same day' practices. Really good stuff, Tom. And I'm surprised. I thought I had to do my job by defending the status quo."

"Well, let's hope the good times continue and the research shows we made a good choice. That's really a good idea. I like it. Who is the young man who thought of this idea on his own?"

"Gary Riesling. Bright kid."

"I'd like to talk to him sometime. He may have some other ideas we should be considering."

"I'll tell him of your interest." Henry stood up and said, "Thanks for pushing me, Tom."

"Never mind that, sounds like you and your faculty are doing the hard work."

They shook hands and Dr. Dunstan left. Tom left the door open and sat back down at his desk. 'Did Ron fall off the edge of the world?' he thought.

CHAPTER 36

Monday, February 17

The next day Tom was standing in the kitchen eating a bowl of cereal for breakfast when Sandra came in. "I thought you had left," she said.

"Just went out for the paper," he replied. "Why? You got a date or something?"

"Yes, darling. My boyfriend is on the way over. I promised him you'd be gone by now," she said sarcastically as she got a fruit cup.

"Well, then, I think I'll just stick around for a while. I want to see what this guy's got that I don't"

"Well, for starters, he doesn't mope around all night thinking about murders and all that."

"Was I that bad?"

"You asked me three times who the lead actor was in that movie we watched last night."

"He wasn't very impressive."

"It was Russell Crowe. He's an Oscar winner, babe."

"I was distracted."

"I know. Tell me what's going on. You have been unusually quiet about this. Normally you talk my ear off. This time it's more 'Mum's the word'."

"We're stuck, you know. I think I've told you everything I know about it. Ron's trying to find a way to get the DNA matched in the military record system. The old guy is laying around eating up resources with no hope of recovery and that resident I told you about, Ben Nealy, has talked to Jeremy Hitchings, the hospital lawyer raising concern whether we would be aiding and abetting a murder if we make this guy DNR. I mean this is a nightmare. It's a wonder that Sam hasn't been all over me."

"Remember you saved his ass on a murder once. He's just smart enough to stay out of the way."

"That was completely Ron, as you recall. Took me by surprise although Sam doesn't know that. I think I could probably ride this out a while if I only knew what Ron was doing?"

"Did you call him?" Susan asked reasonably.

" I called the station once. Left a message."

"He'll call when he has something, right?"

"Yeah, that's right. But in the meantime my anxiety is growing by the minute."

"Buck up, soldier. Get back to work." Sandra took the empty cereal bowl from him and put it in the sink.

"Oh, yeah. That's right, I gotta get out of here so your boy friend can come."

"Not without a kiss," she said.

Tom sat in his Ford F-150, making his way down the I-75 by staying in the middle of the pack. He was reminded how a flock of birds together became a complex system of their own, swerving through the sky and avoiding all obstacles with ease. He knew that such flocks, as well as swarms of bees and schools of fish, operated on very simple rules: stay close, match speed and maintain position. As a system, with each bird or fish or bee being apart of the larger organization, these flocks never ran into windows like an individual bird might. As long as the individual members remained part of the flock and obeyed the simple rules, all was well.

Somewhat like the 'flock' of cars on the Interstate, Tom thought. Except that there would always be that one guy who didn't want to match speed or keep position, the guy who was speeding and changing lanes and who, ultimately, created circumstances for either a wreck or a major slowdown. Tom had thought in the past about getting a paintball gun to shoot such traffic offenders. Then he could call the police and tell them to seek the car-or cars-with the bright yellow paint splotches on them for ticketing.

Then his phone rang. Clicking on the hands-free button he answered, "Bolling."

"It's Ron. Got a minute?"

"I have nothing to do but avoid the crazies on 75 south."

"Just listen, then. I have found out a whole lot about that DNA database and it is a powerhouse. They've been collecting samples for thirty years and have a great record on identifying otherwise unknown remains."

"Great. Can they match 'Barry'?"

"First of all, I said 'just listen'. Second, they really started collecting samples at enlistment only around 1990."

"Oh-oh."

"Got that right, 'Barry' must be 70, right? That would make him Vietnam Era, if he did actually serve. And they didn't get samples back then."

"So it's a wash?"

"You have that right, my friend. However, I have a new idea and I'm working on that."

"Tell me so I don't worry."

"Not till I have something. And, no worries. Nobody is in any danger. Talk to you soon." And Ron hung up.

"Great," thought Tom. "Closed a door and tells me not to worry. I really should introduce him to Mastone next time he's at the hospital."

CHAPTER 37

Monday, March 16

Tom was looking for Dr. Joshua Newberry, chairman of surgery. They needed to discuss the Match which concluded the day before. Tom was aware that Medicine, Pediatrics and OB-Gyn had filled their quota for the upcoming year and the chairs and residency directors were happy with the results. Tom had not heard from Surgery until he was leaving the hospital that night and walked out with Ike Delaney, residency director in Surgery. Ike told him of the snafu in the surgery office that had accidentally failed to notify the Matching Program of the actual number of slots they were seeking for next year. The program had done very well, matching five of their top eleven candidates but, because of the information error, their sixth position was unfilled. Ike had explained to Tom how he and Sam had spent the afternoon calling around to try to fill that slot but had not succeeded.

Tom knew how critical it could be for a residency program to run short for the full three years of that slot's tenure and he wanted to see if Newberry wanted any assistance in finding a suitable candidate. He started in the usual place at Newberry's office but came up bare. He walked over to the surgical ward and talked with the nurses there but they had not seen him recently. Finally, he walked over to the research wing and found Newberry in his laboratory working on his mouse model of endothelial regeneration.

"Josh, I've been looking all over for you," Tom said perching on a stool near the bench where Newberry was.

"Tom. You might be aware, we have some new communication devices now, called telephones. Allows you to speak to other people from a distance. I have one. It's right over there. And it is turned on," Newberry said without looking up from his work.

"I don't know how I can get enough steps to make Sandra get off my back about exercising if I don't walk all over this place hunting for people."

"You could do like the director and have Diane call people to come to your office." Josh looked at Tom with a little grin.

"That's a great idea, Josh. I've always wanted to be like Mastone. Maybe I'll try that next time."

"Long as you're here. Want to talk about our match results?"

"Yep, I saw Ike as I was leaving last night and he said you ended up one short."

"That's about it. And it was our fault. Secretary actually sent in the match form by fax and cut off the bottom line. Made us look like we only had five slots. Ike is calling several folks he knows at various schools to see if they have unmatched candidates. We didn't find anybody yesterday. I thought maybe you could help, too." Sam laid down his small animal instruments and turned to face Tom. "Specifically, I wondered if you have any contact with the Health Professions Scholarship Program." Newberry was referring to the national program that provides tuition and fee support for candidates to attend medical school who then are military officers in the Ready Reserve and have a commitment for active duty time repaying the scholarship on a year-for-year basis. These students are supported while in state or private medical schools and many of them are allowed to complete residency training before repaying their military obligation.

Newberry went on, "And maybe you know somebody at USUHS," speaking about the Department of Defense's medical school in Bethesda. Students at USU are active duty officers, O-1 in rank, and receive full pay in addition to tuition-free schooling. The two programs are federally funded to provide a pipeline of medical, dental and nursing professionals to the armed services but allow graduates to take residency outside the military before beginning their military pay-back.

"Actually, I know somebody in both places. My contact at the HPSP is several years old and may not be active but one of my good friends went to USUHS just last year. What do you want me to tell them?" Tom was pleased to be asked to help.

"Well, you know our program and what the University has to offer so you could prime the pump if they have someone. But, mostly, I think that either Ike or I should call the candidate, so if you can get names and numbers, I'd appreciate it."

"OK. I'll go get at it right now, How's the research going?"

"All right, but very slow. And the older I get the less good I am at operating on these little buggers," he said indicating the two mice playing in the bottom of their cage."

"I know what you mean. I wouldn't want to try to do a hip replacement on them, either," Tom said giving an exaggerated shiver as he left the lab.

Tom decided to take the stairs and one floor down he met one of the physician assistants from internal medicine. They stopped for a short chat and as Tom continued on down he suddenly had an idea about what to do about 'Barry'.

He spent the next hour in his office on the phone, first trying to reach Gary Eisenberg at the HPSP but he had left the organization and then calling the Uniformed Services University of he Health Sciences. USUHS is in Bethesda adjacent to the new Walter Reed Military Hospital and graduates more than a 100 students each year. These students have a military obligation for the absence of tuition and a debt-free medical education but not all of them do their internship and residency programs in the military. They enter the match like everyone else and sometimes miss out on getting a slot when the music stops.

Tom found his friend in the admissions office and asked, "Did everyone in the graduating class match?"

Harper Thompson said, "Tom, I don't think we've failed to match everyone in any year since I've been watching. You know our graduates are among the top in the nation, top half in entering GPA, top half in MCAT scores. And they only look better after four years in our system."

"I know all about the school, Harper. I have actually lectured there. Once. Years ago. I'm calling for a friend. We have an opening for a first year resident in surgery."

"Understood, General. And I would like to help but our chickens all have a roost for July."

"Glad to hear it, Thanks anyway." Sam sat for a moment after finishing the call and then buzzed Mary on the intercom.

"Yes sir?"

"Mary, could you see if Richard Abert could come by the office now?"

"Yes sir."

Tom pulled up his phone and wrote a quick text to Newberry. "Sorry. No luck."

*   *   *

"Tom," Dick Abert said at the doorway ten minutes later. "You wanted to see me?

"Yes. Come in, Dick. I have an idea I would like your opinion on."

Abert took the 'dignitary' chair as Tom indicated and Tom stood at the front of his desk. "I know we have some beds that get occupied by patients that are difficult to place on occasion."

"Is this about that 'Barry' guy?"

"No. Well, somewhat. Actually his situation got me to thinking, 'what if we had our own sort of 'placement' for such patients'?

"You mean open our own nursing home?"

"Not at all. But I seem to remember that you told me the medical residents were griping last year about having such patients on their teaching services, right?"

Abert nodded, "Yes, that's a theme I hear a lot from the residents. But it's not just us. They have the same issue at the University and at the VA. And they have a point."

"And I agree. What if we could set up a ward-or half a ward-somewhere for patients who have met their maximum hospital benefit and where they could be cared for while we work on their difficult placement issue?'

"Sounds interesting, Tom, but where are those actual beds and who is going to 'take care of them' as you say?" Abert sounded positive in spite of the negative questions.

"Well," Tom said a little self-satisfied. "I know the answer to the first question and I'm looking to you to answer the second."

"Let's hear your half first," Abert said.

"OK. The simple answer is 'they are already in those beds'. You have about 6 or so patients on three different wards that are simply awaiting placement. Waiting for a nursing home bed to open up. Meantime, they are sitting in a bed that costs us acute care resources and we won't get paid for that."

Tom waited a moment while Abert mulled the concept and before he could speak Tom went on, "But we can't really leave them there because the staff and all is what makes that an acute bed. But I can move people and resources around to put all those beds together on, say a half ward and staff it at observation levels and we could save some money."

"Where would that ward be?" Abert was seeing right to the heart of the matter in his opinion. If the beds were taken from the medicine wards, he would have a smaller empire.

"I'm not ready to commit on that but I know there are several such patients on surgical wards, as well. So, I'm confident that Sam would like the idea, too."

"Well, I'm not sure about the 'answer' to the first part. What do you think I'm supposed to come up with for the second part?"

"My idea is we need a generalist and a PA to care for them. Let's say I could persuade Roslyn to help me create a staffing model for Observation and that Sam will let me spend some money to adapt the space then we would have to have a physician seeing the patients until they are placed but a PA could provide most of the daily care that nurses would want from the residents or the physician."

"But you would want that staffing to come from Medicine, right?"

"Of course. We want an internist providing that care. I would try to get the PA position from elsewhere or I can go to Sam for some new money.'

"And how do you see this functioning, exactly?" Abert said, more than a little intrigued.

"Don't know all the details. I've only been thinking about this for an hour or so. But I would imagine a team approach. Led by the physician with a PA, an engaged head nurse, and a dedicated social worker. Ward teams see a patient ready for discharge that is awaiting placement and they send a consult to the team. Twenty-four hour service happens. Patient is seen by the team and transfer is made if appropriate."

"Who decides what is appropriate?"

"The team. With guidance from their 'customers', mainly you and Sam."

"If I were to say, 'yes' to this idea. What next?"

Tom shook his head and shrugged his shoulders before answering. "I will have to get Sam on board which should not be hard. I'll ask Beverly to run up some numbers on what it is costing us to do things now. Once Sam buys off I will go to Roslyn and make the best pitch I can. I really think she will go along with moving the long-term care off acute wards."

"OK. I think it might just work. Let me talk with Bruce and Heidi before anything goes public."

"Certainly. Let's talk some more when we have more information."

After Abert left Tom sat at his desk and thought about the many times major problems had allowed him to develop new solutions. Not everything is fixed by going faster.

CHAPTER 38

Tuesday, March 17

The Morning Meeting was missing a major player. Roslyn Burke was attending a local nursing convention as a keynote speaker. Alena Preston, her executive assistant, had no issues to discuss and, briefly, Tom thought the meeting would be concluded in record time. But Sam wanted to hear about an issue regarding a delayed discharge from the Surgical Service that had come to his attention.

Tom and Beverly knew about the issue but since it was predominantly an issue with the discharge planning of the patient and that area of care was under the jurisdiction of the nursing service. So, they let Alena make the explanation.

Her description of the events initially started as something that was not properly handled by the surgeon. A quick look at Tom who gave a minimal shake of his head led her to modify the string of events thereafter.

Alena tediously laid out the story; the involved patient was a 68 y/o man who fell off a ladder in his yard cleaning his windows and broke his hip. After successful reduction of the fracture and pinning of the hip he was scheduled for transfer to a skilled nursing facility for rehabilitation. However, on the day of planned discharge his family appeared and requested that he remain in the hospital for acute care rehabilitation.

Discharge was delayed for two days while this alternative was examined and proved to not be appropriate. The patient had no need for acute care; his entire medical need was rehabilitation. The initial plan was reinstituted and he was discharged. Tom had seen numerous cases where family changing their mind at the last moment disrupted solid discharge plans; he knew there was no 'fault' in this case to be laid at anyone's doorstep.

When Sam began to take issue with the discharge planning activity and was about to pivot his focus from 'lost income' to particular nurses, Tom interrupted, "This is one of those circumstances that are unforeseen, Sam. No one could know the family was about to change their mind. I'm sure that the social worker and the nurses on the ward had communicated to the family exactly what was to be anticipated at discharge."

"What can we do to prevent this from happening again?" Sam asked, swiveling his attention to Tom.

"Probably nothing. This case is news to you for some reason but the clinicians have seen cases like this every week, right Alena?"

"Yes, that's right," she admitted.

"Well, we shouldn't have this happening," Sam emphasized with a hand gesture.

"Perhaps the Discharge Planning Group might consider always having an alternative plan," Tom suggested looking at Alena.

"You know the issues with trying to find more than one bed for a patient," she replied starting a small frown.

"Uh huh," he answered flicking his eyes toward Sam at the head of the table. After a beat, Alena grasped Tom's meaning: Sam would take their 'proposal' as a 'fix' for the problem if she agreed.

"But that's a good idea," she said. "Certainly something we can all work together on."

Beverly ducked her head and scratched the back of her neck so that no one could see the grin she could not suppress. Sam nodded at everyone to indicate that the issue was considered resolved.

Tom said, "there may be some problems with the general surgery program for now."

Sam, who did not completely favor the presence of University-affiliated programs at New City, frowned at this and asked, "Why/ What's that all about?"

"Well, they didn't fill their positions in the Match."

"Don't they usually fill?"

"Yes. I don't think this has anything to do with the value of the program. Apparently it was a clerical error that they inadvertently notified the Match of fewer positions than they actually have. They filled all they asked for."

"Is that something Joshua can fix?" Sam inquired, partially interested at that point. "You know, find somebody else."

"He's trying. I looked into a couple of places myself."

Sam looked at everyone else at the table and said, "You know, I never have understood this Match thing. Usually it didn't make any difference since all the positions were filled. Maybe you could tell me more about it." He ended by focusing his attention directly on Tom.

Others at the table sensed dismissal and they rose and exited, leaving Sam and Tom to talk.

"So, what's this match thing all about, Tom?"

"There's a long history going back to the 1950s before either of us was in this business. Back then medical students thought that the way they got matched to training programs was unfair. So changes were made to keep both sides blind and put a unbiased third party in the middle."

"What's the big deal?"

"Graduating students want to get into the best training program for their career. Or they may want to go to a particular part of the country or they're married and both want to have careers in the same city."

"Why is that so hard?"

"Because the universities and hospitals all want the best and the brightest to be part of their training program."

"So, everybody wants the best, what could go wrong?" Sam made this remark with a sly little grin indicating he understood the issue.

"Exactly. So, the National Matching Program has evolved over the years to use mathematical means of matching applicants, meaning graduating medical students, to available training positions."

"Don't people still interview? I remember having some kids in here interviewing."

"Sure they do. That's how both sides get some personal skin in the game. Interviews are late in the fourth year of medical school. But you don't have to interview at a place to apply there."

"That sounds crazy."

"Applications contain all the relevant material on grades, class rank, letters of recommendation and like that. So programs might be interested in someone who didn't make a visit."

"Still sounds pretty complicated."

"Well, the whole thing is actually pretty smooth. After the interview period is over, sometime in February, every training site makes a list of people they would like to have in their program, and the list is ranked from the top applicant to the last."

"Why are places ranking people they don't want?"

"They're not. Last place on a list is still somebody you are interested in having in your program, just not the highest on your list."

"I see. Everybody on the list is acceptable."

"That's right. And the graduates make their own list, ranking the places where they would like to go for training."

"And they don't mention places they don't like, I guess."

"Of course not. And when all is done, the computers in the Matching Program make mathematical pairings of the highest place on a student's list with the highest pace on the training site list. Theoretically, every body gets the best match."

"If it works out that way, how'd surgery get missed this year?"

"The new clerk in Josh's office faxed their list in and didn't realize the paper was two-sided. She only sent the front sheet and left off the rest of their list. They filled all the slots that were recognized but not the one 'on the back' as it were."

"She still got a job?"

"Yep. Josh says she works harder than anyone now. Do you know about the betting?"

"Are you going to tell me there's illegal gambling going on in my hospital?" Sam laughed.

"Every year the faculty make bets on how well they will do according to how far down their list they go before filling all their positions. There is some argument now going on as to whether the surgical service 'filled' the positions they advertised or 'went to the bottom' of their list. Makes a big difference for the bettors and it is unlikely to be resolved."

CHAPTER 39

Friday, March 20

'What a week', Tom thought to himself as he exited the parking facility at New City. This was one of his favorite times of the week, Friday in the going-home traffic. Sitting high up in the Ford F-150, enclosed in the sound-reducing cab he felt insulated from the weekday slings and arrows. He rarely turned on the radio because he enjoyed the time to reflect on events, replay some conversations and chew on things he wish had gone differently. And maybe even play out some future conversations in his head.

He moved comfortably into the flow of traffic heading north on I-75, content for now to forego a more meandering trip through the neighborhoods. Tom liked to see the reawakening of nature in the springtime. Often his drive to or from the hospital would take him through the small neighborhoods where he enjoyed the budding trees and new growth flowers. That drive would wait a month or so to better correspond to the blooming and budding. That relaxing trip would still be needed, he was sure, in another month after the events of this past week.

Tom also enjoyed looking at porches, particularly those with room for rocking chairs. His youth included time at his grandparent's home where the front of the house was covered by a wide and deep porch.

He played in its shadow, drank gallons of Grandma's lemonade sitting on the broad steps after baseball and, later, sitting in the rocking chairs with Grandma talking about Grandpa.

He thought about his idea of the 'observation' ward and how much that idea had morphed into a burgeoning plan since Monday. His discussion with Beverly was interesting in itself. As he had started telling her the answers he had given to Abert, she began to finish his sentences. Beverly clearly thought this was an idea that needed some data support and she was eager to begin that collection activity. She had been so in tune with the idea that she was able to bring Tom a serious analysis of preliminary data by Tuesday afternoon. They had then spent time into the early evening checking figures and even planning a presentation for the director. Tom knew that Mastone was always more impressed with a presentation if it involved graphs, especially if there was a request for finances involved.

Wednesday, Tom remembered, he had been on the ward and ran into Lila Ralston, one of his favorite nurses. On a spur of the moment he asked her sit in the small waiting area on the ward and gave her a thumbnail sketch of the plan to create an 'observation' ward. Lila had given the idea serious thought for a minute or two, had asked important questions about nurse staffing of the area and then smiled at Tom and said, "That's really a good idea for the patients and for nursing." He smiled to himself thinking how his presentation had been strengthened by answering her questions.

Tom knew better than to present his idea to Sam at the Morning Meeting since Roslyn Burke, Chief Nurse and her executive assistant, Alena Preston, would feel sandbagged if that was the first they were hearing of the plan. Tom instinctively knew they would resist and Sam would hesitate. So he had planned his approach in a step-wise fashion beginning with getting Sam Mastone on board first.

Tom remembered the difficulty he had finding time for an hour presentation to Sam. It appeared that the director's schedule was so chopped up during the day that a free hour only occurred during the noon hour when Sam liked to go to the City Club. When Bev couldn't find the time on the schedule Tom had decided it was time for him to get involved. He had gone right to the top of the authority pyramid-Sam's secretary, Diane Ruttiger. She held the director's schedule and made any necessary changes to it. Tom had gone to her desk and made a case for a meeting that day. Diane, who had been with Sam for eight years, knew his schedule and habits as well as anyone.

Diane had indicated to Tom that the choppy schedule of the director's day resulted from Sam asking for some meetings but allowing the other person to set the time. Once she understood the conflict and Tom's real need for the time she made two phone calls as Tom watched. Within five minutes, or possibly less, Diane had rearranged the schedule to give Tom a full hour right after lunch. Tom remembered walking back to his office thinking, 'I really need to stay on Diane's good side.'

And then, maneuvering the F-150 into the left hand lane, Tom recalled the presentation he and Beverly had made to the director. Mastone was comfortable and a little prone to agreement after his luncheon at the Club. Beverly had wisely arranged the presentation to emphasize first the financial hit that occurred when caring for long-term care patients on an acute care ward. With that problem firmly in front of Sam, the presentation of the suggested 'observation ward' became a solution rather than an idea looking for a reason. Tom remembered how Sam had almost jumped at the 'solution' he and Beverly put forth. Naturally, he wanted to assume control and begin to manage the project. Fortunately, Tom had anticipated that reaction and had simply said, "Well, you'll have to get Roslyn and Nursing Service on board. They don't know about this yet."

Tom almost laughed out loud in the traffic with the recollection of Sam's reaction to the idea that he would have to defend some clinical change to the chief of nursing. His mouth opened and shut twice and then he assumed a facial expression of deep thought, after which he had said, "Maybe you should take the lead on this, Tom. I mean it does involve the physicians, too, right?" And, of course, he said that with all the sincerity in the world. Tom also remembered how he had reluctantly agreed, ""You're right. I'll go speak with her right away." He and Beverly left and went to Tom's office before engaging in some high-fives.

Tom was signaling to change lanes for his exit as he recalled his own surprise at Roslyn's support for the idea. Tom had gone to her office to make the presentation and to ask for her support, thinking she would be more at ease on 'her' grounds. He had expected a delay- probably to consult with Alena and maybe the head nurses. But Roslyn had promptly agreed with the idea, "This is a good thing for the nurses. I like it. I will assign Alena to help with the planning." And that was pretty much it. Bingo on the first round. Tom had walked back to his office thinking 'Things don't really go this well. Something's gonna blow up.'

But things did not explode. This very morning at the Morning Meeting, both Sam and Roslyn had mentioned the plan and said nice things about it. Sam had also said something good about the idea as Tom's and Roslyn, bless her little heart, had actually smiled and nodded at him.

Now he needed to get into the weeds of putting the 'good idea' into actual practice. Beverly's data showed him there were other cases in addition to 'Barry' that needed this form of care and he was gratified that he was at least starting the project without significant resistance.

As Tom exited from the interstate his phone rang. He waited to answer until he had completed the turn, then clicked the key on his steering wheel, "Hello, Bolling here."

"Are you home yet?" came the familiar voice of Ron Looney.

"Just about."

"Well, it doesn't matter. I got news." Ron's voice was light-hearted.

"Shoot."

"Don't say something like that to an ole Arkansas boy."

"You are really pumped about something, aren't you, 'ole Arkansas boy'."

"You bet I am. I hit the jackpot on 'Barry'. Family tree and the whole she-bang."

"Start at the beginning."

"Nope. You gotta be sitting down to hear this."

"Ron, I drive sitting down. Talk."

"Well, you need to be sitting down and holding a beer."

"That will be about 12 minutes from now."

"See you there," Ron said, the elation in his voice was noticeable as he disconnected.

CHAPTER 40

Friday, March 20

Twenty-five minutes later Tom and Ron were clicking longneck beer bottles together on Tom's patio. By that time Ron was slightly more subdued but still obviously one happy guy. "So, let me start at the beginning," he said after the first swig on his beer.

"Remarkable," Tom said. ""Is this going to be a habit with you?"

"As I said, in the beginning I was asked to help identify a nameless, homeless man who had no fingerprints." Another swig on the beer. "And he had no teeth and we couldn't get the military DNA bank to help."

"I'm with you so far," Tom said. "And, I might add, I have learned nothing new." He raised his arm and ostentatiously looked at his watch.

"So where do you go with a DNA sample to find a match?" Ron inquired, ignoring the insult. Tom started to shrug a negative reaction but stopped halfway.

"You went all ancestry stuff …?" he exclaimed.

"So, I went all 'ancestry stuff'. I sent the sample to two different sites that would give me familial matches. And I got a hit yesterday." Ron finished his beer and turned it upside down with a frown.

"Oh yeah, you get another one," Tom said hustling inside. Shortly, Ron raised the new bottle and said, "The hit came with names and the names gave me a whole world of information. But where to start on that?"

"Maybe you could try the Army way, with BLUF," Tom said.

"You mean, Bottom Line Up Front?"

"Exactly."

"OK. Your boy was right. I think somebody is trying to kill 'Barry', whose name is probably Eugene, by the way."

"Keep going."

"That was the bottom line."

"Well, go back and fill in the blanks."

"The ancestry database says the DNA we submitted has a sibling. That information led me to check the name and it turns out that the family is somewhat larger than even the database knows."

"How'd you get all that information?" Tom asked.

"Not hard, actually. Because this family is rich and famous."

"'Barry's' family?" Tom asked, shocked.

"Eugene."

"Eugene's family is rich and famous? Who are they?"

"The Cooke family of Pittsburgh, that's who."

"Never heard of them."

"Well, they are still rich and they are famous in their circle of rich people."

"And you found all this out, how?" Tom was really curious.

"Gene and I have been reading newspapers and People magazine and tabloids all day, that's how."

"How does all this have anything to do with "Barr … Eugene?""

"The way Gene and I put this together the family story starts with a great-great-grandfather of Eugene in Pennsylvania in the 1850s. Seems he had moved to Pennsylvania from Connecticut to find land for farming. A friend of his back in Connecticut told him that the New Haven bankers were starting a company to explore for oil in that same area. The land was not very good for crops and so Great Grandpa was able to buy a significant chunk of acres, which he later traded to the new Seneca Oil Company for shares in the company and its product. This put him in on the bottom of the oil business. He initially used income from the shares to buy a supply store that catered to the drilling business and did quite well but within a decade or two the drilling business tapered off and he sold the store and began to live on his investment. By the time he died his investment was worth millions.

"The next two generations of Cooke's became players in the industry and helped to encourage and build rail lines for transporting the oil. With those investments and his stock in the oil business, Eugene's grandfather, sold out to Big Oil for hundreds of millions. And the family has been without need of 'working employment' ever since. The Cooke family has supported the arts with donations to the Carnegie Museums, the Pittsburgh Symphony and was a major contributor to renovations in the Opera House a few years back."

Tom made some circular motions with his hands.

"Moving on," Ron responded. "Eugene was born in 1946 as part of the Baby Boom. By then the family was high society in Pittsburgh and all their doings got coverage in the society columns. He was called 'most eligible bachelor' before he was twenty but then mention of him stops. Nothing in the papers since except to mention his name as a survivor when his mother died a few years later."

"Fascinating, Ron. But why does all that make you think somebody is trying to kill 'Bar . .' Eugene"?

"Only for the number one reason for murder. Money."

"This old guy?"

"Yes. The papers were all full of it last year. But let me finish setting the stage. Eugene's mother died in '67 but his father remarried in 72."

"I'm seeing a potential conflict … "

"Absolutely. You would make a great detective if you ever give up doctoring. Right! There are other children from the second marriage."

"And that brings us to the money motive?"

"Yes. The old man died last year; second wife died several years before. Somehow the papers got wind of the details about the will." Ron stopped his narration and looked at his empty bottle.

"No more beer 'til you get to the point."

"The will, the only will, is decades old and only mentions Eugene."

"The second family is left out?"

"Exactly!"

"And you think they are trying to kill our 'Barry' to get at the millions?"

"Don't you?" Ron asked with a surprised look on his face.

"Well, yes, it's certainly suspicious . . ."

"Its more than that to me and Gene. It's a flaming sky-high monument to Motive. We don't have anything else on the radar with motive. We have some work to do on the Means and Opportunity, but we'll get there."

"What're y'all doing?"

"Gene and I are spending the weekend looking into some things. I'm going to get a warrant for some bank and credit card records. By Monday, I will know whether any siblings are innocent of not."

" I thought you didn't like getting warrants."

"I don't but had to have this one. I asked the Assistant District Attorney to push this one at the federal level since this may cross state lines."

"Very clever, you will make an excellent detective yourself, and you can have another beer."

"Are you gonna call that resident with the high bar of suspicion and let him know he was right? I mean after you get the beer."

"It's a low bar and that call comes after you show me some proof."

CHAPTER 41

Tuesday, March 24

Ron and Gene spent two days pursuing the strong lead they had about the Cooke family and the connection to Eugene, formerly known as 'Barry'.

Captain Arne Thorason had been interested, or seemed to be at least, in Ron's explanation of the situation.

"Huh." Arne had said when Ron explained that there was a probability that a patient at New City was the target of assassination. Captain Thorason, or 'Thor' behind his back, was prone to the use of that word to express a question, surprise, growing disinterest or dismissal. His meaning was all in the inflection and that was exceptionally subtle. There were those in the Dick Pen, the office area for detectives, who believed there was no variation in inflection and that Thor was always basically disinterested unless the conversation involved an arrest.

Thor ran a good ship; the Homicide Division under his leadership was responsible for obtaining 60% closure of their cases with an arrest. Ron Looney had found that his own style of working meshed very well with Thor's leadership style. Over the years Ron had few instances where he had been the recipient of the famous 'Look' from Thor. The 'Look' originated from Thor's background as a middle linebacker in college as he assessed the offensive set and directed the defense. The

'Look' now assessed the personal worth and rationale for existence of anyone who failed to meet 'the standard' in Homicide. That 'standard', of course, was set by Arne Thorason.

Ron rather enjoyed working for Thor. He remembered when he had been offered a leadership role in the Air Force and found that he was most uncomfortable telling others how to do their job. Or, as it sometimes was, just to do their job. Thor's methods of leadership involved a good deal of personal respect for the detectives even when they exhibited highly variable work habits and approaches. As long as the necessary boxes were checked, no laws were broken outright and no one died who shouldn't have, Thor was not interested in how the right end came about.

Ron had gone to Thor for some insight into getting a federal warrant. Ron felt certain that Eugene's existence was a threat to someone in the Cooke family and they would have to cross state lines to get to him, ergo federal case. But neither Ron nor Gene had ever applied for a federal warrant and they did not want to make a misstep.

"Huh," was Thor's initial response to the question. Then, after a moment's pause with no further input from either Ron or Gene, he went on. "Not especially different. Go to the District Attorney's office and ask for help on a federal warrant. Same detailed case, same request but it will have to go to a federal judge. That's all."

And they did. Gene laid out the case from documents that Tom had provided. He noted the oddness that Ben had recognized: the very expensive, and high potency, whiskey in the first instance and the use of intravenous heroin in a non-drug user in the second. In those instances he felt comfortable writing the case and posing the relevant questions but the third instance was harder for him.

"Listen," he said to Ron working at the other desk, "I'm not sure what to write about this SUX stuff."

"Well, I'm not either. You chose that part of the application."

"Yeah. But maybe we could get a little better understanding of this stuff. I don't even know where you get it."

"Tom said they use it at the hospital"

"I'm calling him for help."

"Go for it. I'm having my own lot of fun trying to word this application to be sure we get access to all the financial records we need."

Tom was more than happy to help Gene understand the use of SUX. He said, "It's a drug commonly used in surgery. When we put someone to sleep for surgery we also need their muscles to be relaxed. That's really important in abdominal or joint surgery but other kinds, as well."

"So, there's a lot of it around in the hospital."

"Probably not 'a lot', but a good amount, sure."

"Is it kept locked up?"

"Almost all succinylcholine is used by anesthesiologists and they keep all their drugs and stuff locked up."

"Where?"

"Somewhere around the operating room, I think. If you want to know specifics about New City I can ask for you."

"I don't really know, Tom. I mean our warrant needs to outline exactly where we would go look for the stuff and that would include how someone might get it in the first place. You said, 'almost all' is in the operating room. Where is the rest of it?"

"There is always a vial in the ICU in case we need to intubate someone."

"Intubate as in … "

"Red rubber tube in the throat so we can put them on a ventilator. We actually paralyze them for a few minutes while we do that."

"Is that vial locked up, too?"

"Absolutely."

"That kinda closes the door, then. And locks it," Gene said.

"And you don't think it came from New City, anyway, do you," Tom stated.

"Not any good reason to think that right now. Seems more likely it came from somewhere else. Maybe a drug store?"

"I don't believe any drug store would stock SUX. They don't have any reason to be dispensing it."

"Where do the hospitals get it?"

"From suppliers like pharmaceutical companies."

"Direct?"

"I think so. What do you mean by that?"

"Is there a middleman, a distributor or someone like that in the chain?"

"Probably. I really don't know but I can get an answer from our Pharmacy. They order for us."

"That would help, thanks."

"Sure. I'll call you back shortly."

Tom had contacted the pharmacy and returned Gene's call within 15 minutes. To his surprise, it turned out those hospitals in the entire northeastern part of the country got their SUX from the same place, a single distributor in Illinois.

Gene took this information and felt a little more informed as he finished his part of the application in short order.

"Coffee?" he asked of Ron.

"Yeah, sure but not here. I gotta stretch my legs. Let's go down the street."

As they passed the door to Arne's office they saw him at his desk giving a heavy folder The Look. They quickened their pace so as not to get involved.

CHAPTER 42

Tuesday, April 7

Under most circumstances, Ron was apprehensive about warrant applications. His past history of arguing with the judge when asked questions about his application had led him to think that judges were opposed to warrants as a rule.

A few years back he had decided to not be involved in any discussion with a judge about his own requests for warrants and had since then relied on one or more of the ADAs to present his case. In preparation for that, Ron developed a pattern of meeting with the ADA for a "pre-application" question and answer period. The ADA would play hard-nosed judge and Ron and Gene would argue their case far away from the judge's chambers. The better ADAs would push the detectives to fill in holes in the case from a legal perspective to the point they were comfortable with the request. The practice added time to the overall process of obtaining warrants but everyone involved went into the application more certain that their best case was being made.

Then Ron would sit in his desk and stay even farther away from the judge's chambers while the application was reviewed. But he sweated every moment of the time, often replaying his discussions with the ADA and critiquing his own thinking and arguments to the point he became convinced that the judge would not only turn down the application but possibly bar him from ever submitting one in the future. The fact that he was successful three out of four times did not change his feelings about the process.

When he did not hear back from the ADA when he thought he should, he and Gene went back to the coffee shop. It was early in the afternoon and Gene wanted to have a doughnut. Gene's interest in eating at all times of the day was a point of amazement for Ron. His partner was always looking for food-and usually getting some-and yet never gained weight. Ron took his cup and sat at one of the back tables, leaning his chair backward on two legs against the wall..

"She does have your cell number, right?" asked Gene unwrapping his pastry.

"Yeah, and I told her I would likely have to get out of the office while we're waiting. Is that a jelly-filled doughnut?"

"Yes, it is my perceptive friend. Strawberry and delicious."

"Speaking of delicious, when are you gonna make a move on Sandra? Every time we go there for lunch she can't seem to stop giving you the eye." Ron brought this subject up primarily to get Gene into a lengthy discussion of why the time wasn't right for him to be dating. But Gene surprised him by saying, "Oh, I already did."

"What? I thought I knew everything you did. What did you ask her?" Ron asked this so emphatically as he leaned forward that his chair slammed the front legs to the floor.

"What do you think? Think I asked her to share a condom? Calm down, man. I just asked her to dinner."

"Dinner. Going to take the waitress out to eat. Thoughtful."

"I was just going to start with coffee but I thought that was too lame."

"And you were right. Why not a movie or a boat ride?"

"Too over the top for first date. I intend to take her to Primavista."

"Fancy. Does she like Italian or is that for you?"

" I think everybody likes Italian food. And wine."

Ron was leaning his chair back against the wall when his phone rang. The ADA was in their office and wanted to talk.

Scant minutes later the three of them sat around Ron's desk. "It did not go well," Sharon, the ADA said. "He was skeptical of the grounds."

"Did you give him the set up the way I wrote it?" Gene asked.

"I played it exactly the way we worked it out. He just didn't like it. Too circumstantial, he said."

"For crying out loud!" Ron's frustration was showing, and he went on, "Of course it's circumstantial at this point-that's why we need the warrant. Dumbass."

"Calm down, Detective. The judge is doing his job. And this is why it is for the best that you don't go to the application hearing."

"What did he say, exactly? What didn't he like?" Gene persisted.

"Well, one thing he mentioned was that we presented no evidence that the family has any idea that Eugene is alive." She hastened to say before Ron could jump in, "And he thought that was sufficient in itself to hold up approving any warrant. He also said the state of Pennsylvania can declare Eugene dead since he's been gone without a trace for more than 7 years. And the family lawyer knows that. Therefore, in the judge's eyes there is very little motive for this family trying to kill him."

"What about the three bizarre attempts?' Does he think that just happened for no reason?"

"He didn't really address that in depth, his basic reasoning was denying that the Cooke family should be investigated."

"I guess those millions to the Carnegie also means something that crosses state lines," Gene pouted.

Sharon, looked at them both before going on, "Plus, as he said, if the guy is Eugene, he isn't dead."

"Not yet!" expressed Ron with a forceful slam of his hand on his desk.

They talked a few more minutes until Sharon and Gene felt that Ron had calmed down. Right after she left, Thor came out of his office and walked over to where the two were sitting.

"I don't agree with the judge's ruling on this but I got to ask, 'Why are you guys still running after this case? You got nothing and the judge just made that official. We do have some other business here, you know."

Ron said, in his most professional manner, "We understand, Captain. And we're ready to do our share. But this smells too funny for us to just walk away."

"Huh." Arne Thorason had a reputation for trusting his detectives 'gut' feelings if no one ended up embarrassed. He looked at Gene and Ron and said, "End of the week," before turning and going back to his office.

CHAPTER 43

Friday, April 10

Tom left the Morning Meeting and walked back to his office with Beverly. "At least we don't spend more than 15 minutes in that meeting," he said quietly.

"Sometimes there are important issues," she countered.

"Yes, I remember. But we never agree in that meeting to do anything except get someone else to go to work on the issue.

"Is that unimportant?"

" C'mon, Bev. Let me vent a little. You're always so positive."

"Oh no I'm not," she replied. "Remember when the Issue of the Day was the failed air conditioner in the Executive Suite? That went on for two days and then we heard about the 'solution' for another week. I was not Ms. Sunshine then."

"OK. That's true. Sorry if I insulted you by suggesting you were the most positive person I know."

"No offense taken." She smiled and left him to enter her office.

Tom's phone was ringing as he entered his office. Picking up the receiver he heard the familiar voice of Ron Looney. "Hey, General, I got news."

"I hope you are not a regular poker player," Tom said.

"What?"

"I mean you have a big tell. You never call me 'General' unless you have something you want from me or you're about to give me bad news."

"Well, this time's it's the bad news variety. The judge turned down my request for a warrant on the Cooke family finances. And Thor is giving me to the end of the week-meaning today. Gene and I have done what we can reading the society pages trying to link one of the siblings with absence from Pittsburgh on the days that Eugene was attacked but we can't make a case."

"Will that mean your investigation cannot continue?"

"It means I likely won't have time or any resources to spend on it like I've been doing. But no, it doesn't mean everything comes to a halt. Have you got anything new I could tell him to get a little more time?"

"I really haven't been up on the ward in several days now, but I don't know that anything's different. Sorry."

"Yeah, well, we may come over and look around anyway. I don't want to shut this down without at least talking to your resident again."

"Ben Nealy."

"That's the one."

"If it will help I'll buy you both a cup of special coffee."

"Deal," Ron said and disconnected.

Tom sat down and leaned back in his chair. His opinion on Ben's diagnosis had slowly shifted in favor of the position the resident had been pushing since before Christmas. There really wasn't a better answer to a reason behind the egregious attacks on 'Barry' than attempted murder. And, now that he knew about the issue with inheritance of millions Tom shared the suspicion of Gene and Ron that the family members were somehow at the bottom of the attempts. Tom didn't relish having the 'case' go cold. But he knew enough from things Ron had explained in the past that suspicions don't go over well in court. There it's more like Dragnet and 'just the facts, m'am,' and the facts they had were few.

He decided to go check in on how Eugene, formerly known as 'Barry', was doing. The new 'observation' area would open on that same ward in just a few days and Eugene Cooke was slated to be one of the first four patients accepted. As Tom stepped off the elevator he noted that Ben and his team were starting their rounds. He didn't want to disturb that function so he nodded briefly to them in passing and went to the nursing station. He stood at the end of the counter for a few minutes, thinking about what else he might uncover to help Ron.

As he stood there he became peripherally aware of the white noise and activity on a medical ward. He noticed the nurses quietly coming and going in their running shoes, scrubs and colorful tops. Nothing like the old days when nurses wore white dresses, white shoes, white hose, and white caps. Tom noticed the food service guy in cap, mask and gown with the squeaky wheeled cart; and the pharmacy technician bringing a basket of medications behind the counter to restock the crash cart. Tom thought there must have been a code recently.

Two nurses sitting at the desk stood up and went down the hall and two others took the empty seats and signed on to the computerized medical record to make their entries. Tom remembered how often he and Sam had discussed getting the bedside stations for the nurses to improve timeliness of notes. Another quality of care issue that was stymied by lack of any evidence trail that could pry loose the necessary funding. With an effort he remembered he was there to see if there was anything he could give to Ron. He looked at Eugene's room to remind himself of the room number just as the food service man came out of the room.

Tom turned to one of the nurses already logged into the computer and asked who was Eugene's nurse on that shift. She replied that she was and Tom indicated he wanted to discuss the man's status. Their discussion was almost immediately cut short and interrupted by alarms coming from Eugene's room. The nurse Tom was talking to bolted toward the room along with three others.

Again Tom stepped back and watched the tableau as if it were in slow motion; personnel dropping their every day duty to respond to an immediate need. As he watched there were three patterns of behavior, those moving toward the room, those standing still or consciously getting out of the way and one or two figures moving in the opposite direction. Time slowed down. Tom knew what was happening in the room and did not need to insert himself. He saw the faculty member assigned to Code Review arrive and slide into the room.

The chatter of calls for medication and notice of intent to use electric shock was audible at the nurses' station but not loud. Tom looked down the hall and noted that the attending team had stopped their movement while Ben and one of the students had joined the resuscitation. After only a few minutes the noise from the room dropped significantly and then stopped for a few beats. Then, slowly, personnel began exiting the room. That could have only one meaning: Eugene was dead. Tom wondered if that fact alone would be useful to Ron. If Ben Nealy was right, whoever was interested in causing the death of Eugene Cooke now had their wish. He pulled out his cell phone to call Ron.

CHAPTER 44

Friday, April 10

Ron answered without a salutation. "Well, I sure hope this is good news."

"He's dead," Tom said, flatly.

"Eugene? When?"

"Right now. Some kind of emergency. I'm on the ward looking at the nurses cleaning up the room."

"Whoa, man. Tell them to stop and get out of there."

"What are you talking about?" Tom said even as he started toward the room.

"It's a crime scene. The guy was murdered. We both know that."

"But the 'crime' occurred weeks ago."

"Just stop everybody. I want to talk to that Ben and anybody else that can tell me what happened in there."

"OK. But this better be quick."

"Funny thing, Gene and I are almost to your parking garage right now." The line went dead.

Tom stuck his head in the doorway to Eugene's room and noted that the cleanup activity had not yet begun in earnest. He spoke quietly to the two nurses still in the room, "Let's leave this alone for a few minutes, OK?"

They looked at him questioningly but got no further information. The nurse assigned to Eugene, looked at the other nurse and shrugged. They left the room without further discussion.

Less than ten minutes later, Ron and Gene walked on the ward. By that time Tom had secured the room and asked Ben and the pulmonologist who observed the code to hang around for a few minutes. When the detectives arrived he introduced the two physicians to Ron. After realizing they were standing in a very public place Ron had then stepped off to the side and somewhat down the hallway to ask them a few questions.

Gene went over to Eugene's room and peered in the door at the jumble of medical wrappings and bandages strewn over the floor. "One of my favorite things in the whole world," he said to Tom.

"What's that?

"A crime scene that's been walked over by fifty people. Do you see anything out of ordinary in there, Doc?"

Tom looked over the room cluttered with bandages, packaging from catheters, used gloves, and other detritus from the code. The crash cart was standing by the bedside with all drawers closed. "Yeah," he said sarcastically to Gene. "Usually most of those drawers are open."

"That's really helpful. Thanks. I'm gonna write that down, doc." came the sarcasm back at him.

Ron walked over and said, "They said this was a slow code, whatever that means, and it was pretty much clockwork. Nobody thought anything was out of order."

"Shall we clean it up then?" Tom asked aware that the nurses were unhappy with the state of affairs and the two responsible for clean up were standing behind the nurses desk, arms crossed watching them closely.

Ron turned to Gene and raised his eyebrows. Gene shrugged and said, "We could box everything up and take it to the lab but remember everyone had on gloves."

"Right. Probably unnecessary." Then after a pause he said to Tom "Let me take a few pictures and then you can clean it up."

While Ron was snapping some photos of the room, Gene walked around the ward and the nurses' station. Nurses tried to get back to their usual activity and Tom spoke to the nurses eager to get on with clean up telling them the room was theirs once Ron had finished with pictures. He then resumed his earlier position at the end of the counter. Waiting for Ron, Tom began to see the slow motion movie again and remembered something odd about the picture. As he was trying to get that straight in his head, Ron walked up and said, "We need to talk about this."

Tom said, "Wait. He didn't belong there."

"Who? Somebody I missed?"

"I saw the food service guy coming out of Eugene's room."

"When?" Ron started looking around the ward.

"Just before the code."

"Well, I should talk to him, too, then."

"That's not the point. Eugene was in a coma. He didn't have a diet ordered. There was no reason for that guy to be in that room."

"Where is this guy now?" Ron asked, looking directly at Tom.

"Gone. He left the ward twenty minutes ago. Right when the code started I saw him pushing that tray delivery cart off toward the elevators."

"You saw him, Tom?"

"Oh yes. The SOB walked right past me as the code was alarming."

"Describe him," Ron said taking out his pencil and pad.

"He was wearing a cap and gown and a mask. I don't know what he looked like, Ron. I was watching everybody run toward the code."

"How tall?"

"uh … "

"Compared to the cart he was pushing?"

"Little less than me, maybe five-ten."

"White?"

"Yeah, I think so."

"Hair?"

"He had on a cap."

"Under the cap. Back of the neck."

"Uh. Dark. Brown, not long."

"Glasses?"

"No."

"Anything else?"

"Yes but I can't put my finger on it. Something funny about him."

"Which way did he go?" Ron asked starting for the elevators himself.

Tom instinctively started for the employee elevators where the food service trays would be handled but Ron turned toward the patient elevators. Tom turned around to correct him and saw the food tray cart sitting across the hallway from the elevators.

"There," he said indicating the cart to Ron.

Ron looked at the doorway right around the corner from where the cart had ended up. A doorway marked 'Exit'. He pushed open the door and started down the stairs with Tom right behind him.

One landing down they noticed the crumpled gown discarded in the corner. At the lobby level the doorway opened into a small recess that would go unnoticed. "These are not the stairs for visitors," Tom explained.

Ron stood at the doorway and said, "So, our guy heads for the elevator pushing the cart, realizes he's at the Visitors elevator so he leaves the cart and heads down the stairs. He ditches the cap and gown and walks out the lobby without anyone paying the slightest attention."

"And he started off by walking right past me," Tom said somewhat bitterly.

"Let's go get that cart and check for fingerprints," Ron said as he headed back up the stairs.

When they came to the crumpled gown, Ron donned some gloves of his own and picked it up noting that the crumpled mass contained the cap and gloves worn by the man pushing the food cart. "Damn," Ron said. "He wore gloves. We're not gonna get any prints off that cart." He slid the clothing into a plastic bag.

Back on the floor, they looked at the cart and Ron opened it using his gloves. It held no trays, just empty slots. On the bottom lay a large bulb syringe.

Tom looked at the syringe and said, "I bet that's your murder weapon."

"Tell me." Ron said as he removed another plastic bag from his pocket and inserted the syringe.

"He probably shot 'Barry' full of air with that."

"Will that kill you?"

"Big enough bubble, yes it will."

"How would he do that?"

Tom thought for a minute and said, "He had a central line."

"Explain, please."

"'Barry' . . uh, Eugene had an intravenous line in his subclavian vein. That's a big vein right under the collar bone. If somebody shot a big bubble of air into that it would kill him in just a minute or two."

"How easy is that to do?"

"Depends. If the nurses who take care of that line have taped the lines together, it could be hard. Otherwise just open the line, push in the air and reconnect. Nobody would notice."

"Anybody use those lines in the resuscitation?'

"Probably, if they were giving medications. Why?"

"I need to talk to the first one in the room." Ron made this semi-order as he abruptly turned and headed back toward the ward.

"The nurse?"

"Yes. The first one in the room."

They returned to the ward and Tom found the nurse assigned to Eugene's care still in the hospital room, cleaning up the last remnant of the code. Tom made a brief introduction and Ron asked, "Were you the first in the room?"

She indicated that she was and he went on and asked her carefully to re-think her actions. She recalled putting the head of the bed down and clearing the intravenous line for medications.

"Anything odd about that line?" Ron asked.

She shook her head at first but then stopped, looked at Tom and said, "Yes. I always tape the lines together. Even for this man who wasn't moving. I do it to keep them from working apart."

Tom nodded in agreement. The nurse turned back to Ron and said, "But they weren't taped any more. When I was getting them ready for the code, they weren't taped together anymore."

"Could someone else have removed that tape before you got there?" Ron pushed.

"No, sir. Absolutely not. I was the first one in the room."

CHAPTER 45

Monday, April 13

Monique Song made the first incision to start the autopsy on Eugene Cooke shortly before mid-morning. Tom and Ron and Gene had gathered in her office just before that to hear her explain what she was going to do and what she had already learned about the death of Eugene Cooke.

Tom had alerted her to the probable cause of death on Friday after he and Ron found the large syringe and heard the nurse's testimony about the lack of taping on the joint to the central line. Monique's personal experience as a Medical Examiner before coming to New City provided her with both background and experience in a number of unusual and seldom used techniques of autopsy. After hearing Tom's explanation on Friday, she had immediately gone to the ward and ordered a post mortem CT scan of Eugene. She had then also accompanied the body into Radiology in order to quell any upset nerves about having a dead person in their domain. She remained in the room with the body during the procedure and afterward accompanied Eugene to the morgue.

Monique also insisted that the digital images from the exam be sent to her computer account for review and then she had spent the bulk of the evening studying the films and reading about fatal air embolization. When she gathered the detectives together in her office

Monday she had a short presentation for them about what happens when air enters the circulatory system in large amounts complete with images from the internet and from Friday's CT of Eugene Cooke.

She was completely convinced from the CT scan results and her reading and investigation that Eugene had died acutely from an air embolus, and she successfully transmitted this certainty to Tom and the detectives even before proceeding to open the body. After making the usual 'Y' incision and removing the chest plate, Monique performed a specific maneuver to corroborate the cause of death. She used an aspirometer to suck out the contents of the right atrium once the chest was open. The aspirometer she used was one from the pulmonary ward normally used by patients after an operation to help them prevent pneumonia. She simply disconnected the mouthpiece and attached a low-pressure vacuum. As Monique turned on the vacuum and increased its pull, the other three observers each took deep breaths as the inner chamber began to fill with a frothy, bloody fluid. She aspirated until there was no further fluid and indicated that she was able to pull out over forty milliliters of frothy fluid.

"The CT scan didn't lie," she said, setting the aspirometer aside.

"You have seen irrefutable evidence that this man died from a large air embolus, probably blocking coronary arteries. And I am prepared to testify to that in court."

"That may be necessary, doctor," said Ron. "But now we know we are dealing with an active murder and we have additional work to do, starting with Thor but also going back to the judge."

"Active murder?" queried Tom. "Is there another kind?"

"Oh yes," said Monique and Ron at the same time. They smiled at each other and he deferred to her.

"There are several cases, somewhat like Eugene here, where an event, usually a shooting, was known to occur but the victim did not die. The legal charge to the shooter was Malicious Wounding or something like that. Then years later, the victim dies from complications of the original shooting and the shooter is arrested and charged with homicide. This case is different because he didn't die from the SUX paralysis and hypoxia and brain damage. He died from a new insult-the air embolus. So it's active, not delayed, homicide."

Ron was vigorously nodding his agreement. "Although," he said, looking at Gene, "I don't know that makes our task any easier since the guy responsible for both events has gotten away."

Gene said, "But we should get a reprieve from Thor to keep working the case."

Monique turned back to the body and began to extract the heart and lungs from the chest cavity.

The detectives were about to excuse themselves when Monique said to them and to Tom, "I'd like you to look at something I didn't know how to interpret." She called their attention to Eugene's left shoulder where a faint outline was present. Monique said, "I'm sure it's a tattoo, Looks almost like it's been scratched off in places. I didn't recognize it but I don't think it's a gang tat."

All three men bent over the shoulder and Gene quickly said, "Don't know," and backed out of the way. As Ron and Tom stared at the blurred lines the image seemed to become clearer. It appeared to have the shape of a shield, possibly a black shield, and a centered profile of an eagle's head.

Almost at the same moment, the two men looked up at each other and said, "Ranger!"

CHAPTER 46

Monday, April 13

"Cap'n?" Ron said inquiringly while standing outside Thorason's door.

Arne looked up and noticed the big grin on Ron's face. "You got something, didn't you?"

"Came within a whisker of catching the guy. He got away but I'm pretty sure we had eyes on and we will get him."

"Caught him doing what?"

"Oh, right. In the act of killing the old dude at New City."

"So now it's a murder?"

"Absolutely, Cap'n. I just came from the autopsy. Clear case of Murder One."

"Gene on board?"

"Yes, sir."

"What do you need?"

"The warrant."

"Huh."

"Gene's working on updating it and we've got a meeting with the ADA in about an hour."

"Huh." This time Arne broke eye contact and returned to reading the material in front of him. Ron took that as a sign of both agreement and dismissal. When he got back to his desk, Gene was typing away at the addendum to the warrant application. Ron sat at his desk and opened the middle right-hand drawer.

"If you're going into the candy, I want some, too," Gene said without taking his eyes off the typing.

"Here you go," Ron said lofting a miniature Mounds Bar over the desk.

"Thanks."

"How much longer?"

"Fifteen or twenty minutes. This is really juicy."

"Candy bar or your writing?"

"Actually both."

Ron left him alone to finish the application and sent a text to the ADA confirming their meeting. Within a few minutes, Sharon replied with agreement. With nothing to do for a few minutes Ron started paging back through the papers he had collected and realized he had not printed out the pictures he took of Eugene's hospital room after the code. He pulled them up on his phone and sent them to his Homicide.gov email address. When they arrived he sent them to the printer in the corner. Gene was just finishing his typing when Ron came back with the pictures. As Gene sent his document to the printer Ron said, "I need more coffee. I sure don't want to make a habit of starting every day in the autopsy room."

"I agree on both points."

They bundled all their material together and headed down the back stairs.

Sitting with their coffee and doughnuts at a back table in the coffee shop, Ron mentioned a concern he had about the case to Gene, "I just don't see the food cart as a 'spur of the moment' thing."

"You think he planned that? How? 'Specially if we're right and he was in Pittsburgh."

"I don't know. It just seems a little too 'arranged', you know."

"You're thinking he had help. An insider?"

"Maybe. I don't know. Tom thinks he just found that cart sitting on the ward and used it as a prop."

"Why doesn't that feel right?"

"I've been up in New City several times on the wards and I don't remember seeing carts like that, especially empty ones, just sitting in the halls."

"How would you know if they were empty?"

"Fair point. I just don't remember seeing them around at all."

"What does Tom say about that?"

"Actually, he's not troubled at all. Says he sees the carts left around the hospital all the time. Food service leaves them there to use later for tray pick-up. And it's an irritant to him. He wants them off the ward. He says he has spoken to the food service people about it and they'll clean it up for a while and then it happens again."

"So, he's not troubled by the 'spur of the moment' thing?"

"Not about the cart. He's more concerned about the syringe."

"Yeah. You mentioned that before. What's his worry there?"

"He says they don't use those much. Apparently they're for irrigating bladders and such."

"Ouch. I don't need to be thinking about that."

"I don't want to think about that either. Maybe it will come out in the wash when we catch this guy."

"Did Thor give us a deadline?"

"No. But he did say 'Huh' about the warrant. So, we have that going for us."

Gene worked his way through the last of his doughnut and took a swig of coffee. "I can't do the long night thing tomorrow."

"May not have to. Why, is this the Big Date?"

"See, this is why I don't tell you about my social life. This is the second date."

"Really? How'd she like Primavista?"

"She liked everything that evening very well, thank you. Enough that the second date was an easy question."

"So, you want to double with me and Meg some night?"

"I think I would rather have a root canal. Are you gonna finish that doughnut?"

Later, sitting in their office and waiting for word from the ADA, each of them became bored and finally Gene asked, "If Tom isn't worried about the cart, what does he think about the surgical cap and gown?"

Ron shrugged. "Somehow it also doesn't seem to bother him that a civilian off the street could get into those. He said the doctors' dressing room is clearly labeled and is not locked. It's in a back hallway where the civilians aren't supposed to be but it's not hidden and anyone could get in there. They don't restrict the access to employees because they allow outside surgeons to come in periodically to help with special cases. Guy could walk in, change into scrubs without anyone thinking it odd. Plus there's mask and caps and gloves everywhere."

"Huh."

"Yeah, that's what Thor said."

Gene decided to see if the bulb syringe was listed on Amazon.

It was almost five o'clock when the ADA called them. "You guys owe me dinner," she said by way of opening.

"You got it?" Ron said excitedly. "Steak dinner anywhere you want."

Gene said, "We got it?"

Ron nodded and took down a few notes from Sharon and said again, "Steak dinner, I promise. Gene said he would pay." And then he quickly hung up.

"Funny, man, but I would be happy to pay if this gets us what we need." Gene said, rubbing his hands together.

CHAPTER 47

Tuesday, April 14

When Tom had both a name and proof of military service he went to work to obtain Eugene's military service record. Since he was not a direct family member of the deceased, he needed to have authorization of some sort to access the file and any access was likely to be hampered by the National Personnel Records Center in St. Louis not being aware of Eugene's death. If the veteran is presumed alive, the Records Center limited access to the files to the veteran him or herself. Even if the Center were notified of Eugene's death access would thereafter be limited to next-of-kin.

Tom called the chief of staff at the Cincinnati VA Medical Center for some assistance. He was put in touch with a nice woman in the Medical Records section to whom he explained his dilemma. As he put it, New City was caring for an unfortunate veteran, a former Ranger, who had developed serious medical problems and the treatment team thought it was likely that he may have been exposed to Agent Orange during the Vietnam War. He mentioned he would be trying to get the man's service record but he needed more information than just the name. Tom suspected that Eugene might have visited the VA Medical Center at some time and they would have completed all due diligence on identifying him and validating his veteran status.

The lady in Medical Records was more than helpful. She quickly put Eugene's name into their system and found he had actually been seen in the last year or so at the VAMC. She was able to provide Tom with a Social Security Number and a Service Number. Tom thanked her profusely and hung up with a plan in mind. It was only later, in the truck heading home that day when he realized he should have asked for a copy of the VA medical record, as well.

Tom then contacted a former aide of his from active duty times who just happened to currently hold a responsible position at the National Records Center. They had enjoyed a short chat about their memories of past service and then Tom asked for a favor.

"Sure," the former aide replied, "anything legal and I'll be all over it."

"Thing is, I'm not sure of the legality."

"Oh oh. What are you needing?"

Tom quickly ran through the history of the man he now knew as Eugene Cooke of Pittsburgh, PA. After emphasizing the suspicious nature of the three incidents that each ended with Eugene in a New City hospital bed, Tom tried to emphasize the criticality of the record as well as the need to by-pass the next-of-kin.

"So you think something in this man's military experience put him off the rails but now his family is trying to murder him?"

"Well, that's a rather blunt way of putting it, but factually correct."

"Why do you think the service record is going to help you?"

"Actually, I'm not certain. From all sources we can obtain, this guy served as a Ranger in Vietnam. We are nearly 100 percent certain that the family is unaware of his presence or activity in the service and are of no assistance to us. It's my gut instinct that he left active duty and fell off the edge of the world. I'm hoping the service record would give us a clue."

"Will it make a difference in your treatment or possible outcome?"

"Great question, Howie. My answer is it probably will not."

Following this disclosure there was a short silence on the other end of the line before Howie said, "Do you have more than a name?"

Tom supplied the SSN and Service Number and home town of Pittsburgh and then waited.

"I'll see what I can do, General."

"I appreciate that, Howie. Be in touch."

Then Tom had leaned back in his chair and thought, "C'mon, Eugene. Give me a little help here."

CHAPTER 48

Wednesday, April 15

om was reviewing the minutes of the Pharmacy Committee in his office around mid-morning. He had enjoyed his morning Black Eye Americano somewhat more than usual because Sam was out of the hospital and that allowed Tom to run the morning meeting. Occurrences like that were fewer than Tom anticipated because Sam was a conscientious executive and was rarely ill. Further, when he was away at meetings like the American College of Healthcare Executives annual gathering, Tom usually attended the same meeting. But this day found Sam away from the city on personal business and Tom in the chair at the head of the table.

Consequently, the meeting was short and quite to the point. No matters for discussion meant no discussion and everyone left the Conference Room just seven minutes after eight o'clock. Tom returned to his office and started on the pile of Committee meeting minutes that he needed to read and sign before they were circulated.

He looked up at the brisk knock and is his doorway saw Monique Song standing there with her usual inscrutable facial expression. Tom had wondered when he and the detectives left the autopsy room so quickly on Monday if she might have been annoyed. Certainly, she did not seem so now. He smiled and waved her in and offered her the choice of various seating. She chose the straight chair beside his desk.

Tom opened the discussion, "I guess you've finished the autopsy on Eugene."

"Yes. Very interesting from a variety of viewpoints."

Tom initially thought this comment indicated that Monique was going to be critical of how she was left alone after cause of death was determined with certainty.

She went on without the slightest hint of irritation. "You can probably guess most of the gross findings. Stage three cirrhosis, general protein-calorie malnutrition, enlarged spleen and extensive cerebral atrophy."

"So," Tom noted, "he wasn't going to ever recover. I think we knew that from the EEG."

"True," She replied. "But that's not the whole cake. Mr. Cooke had another serious problem. He also had gastric cancer. A seven centimeter ugly mass on the lesser curve, eroded through the wall."

"Limited or metastatic?

"He had metastases all over his lungs and several places in the bowel were bleeding. Nurses' notes when he first came in mentioned some bloody stools but that seemed to go away. But the periphery of this stomach tumor was ratty and kinda chewed off." At this, Monique fixed Tom with a solemn stare and waited for a response.

"OK. I give up. What's your point?" Tom asked.

"I thought he had gotten some chemotherapy somewhere. I called the VA Medical Center and sure enough, he had been seen over there. His medical record indicated that he first showed up at the VAMC just a few months ago vomiting blood. Of course they admitted him and did the complete evaluation. Workup made the diagnosis of gastric cancer but he indicated he did not want any treatment. The oncologist's note stressed that he was giving Eugene the information that he could have several more months with treatment and Eugene went AMA."

"Sounds like a pattern."

"And it didn't end there. A few weeks later he showed up again, vomiting blood and seemed like he was more frightened. So he was admitted, transfused and that time he agreed to try the chemotherapy."

"So that time he didn't go AMA?"

"What do you know about treatment for gastric cancer, Tom?"

I know it's a deadly disease. I'm not aware of success with chemotherapy."

"Common drug for this cancer is Xeloda."

"Which is?

"Generic name is Capecitabine."

"I like Xeloda. What's the point?"

"One side effect in about half of the patients is loss of fingerprints."

"No. Really? And we've been thinking he had a big time criminal career."

"The prints are supposed to grow back and I think they were just starting to when he died. But once his skin started to flake off, Eugene apparently gave up. He went AMA from the VA again."

"Ron is going to have to buy drinks for a year!"

"Why?"

"Oh," Tom said smiling at her. "I think I'll bet him the cause was medical and not criminal."

"I think I would like a piece of that action," Monique smiled.

"Only if you can keep from smiling."

CHAPTER 49

Wednesday-Thursday, April 15-16

Gene Novalchek was actually early to work on that Wednesday morning. As usual he was wearing a tie that Ron was quite positive he had not seen before. It perfectly matched Gene's subdued plaid Brooks Brothers suit. He had brought a cup of coffee with him and carefully set it down on his desk before removing his coat and it arranging on a hanger he took from his bottom drawer.

Ron watched all this with more than modest interest, He thought the show was primarily to get his attention and spark discussion about the events of the night before. They had spent most of the previous afternoon using their warrant to collect pre-determined slices of the Cooke family financial records. Bank statements, loan applications, ATM activity on credit and debit cards and direct charges on the cards, as well. The records they had requested spanned the time from the month before Eugene's first admission to New City to the week after his death. That request had produced a sizeable pile of paper and access to even more digital information.

When their first, shallow dive into the information did not find anything remarkable, they had become aware that the review would take many hours and Gene decided to step out of the process at that time.

"Listen, partner. You can do what you want but I've got a date and I don't want my mind filled with numbers," he had said and Ron had waved him out the door and also gone home early. Better to be well rested for the effort the next day, he had reasoned.

So, as Gene waltzed into the Dick Pen Wednesday morning, Ron watched the performance appreciatively before commenting. "You certainly look chipper and well rested this morning."

"I am. I am. I am." came the cheerful answer.

"So, I guess the date ended early for you to be so rested."

"You go right on thinking that, my friend. Where do you want me to start?"

"Let's take a minute and re-think our approach, OK? We now know that our boy Eugene has two siblings. I'm not sure if that's more reason to suspect one or both of them or not but I really do think everything we know points a strong indicator at the Cooke family. So let's brainstorm how they could've done the deed on old Eugene."

"I thought about that a little last night and … "

"Oh ho. So the date was not all that intriguing?"

"I thought a little about that last night as I was driving over to get Sandy," Gene said with a little exaggeration on each word. "Pittsburgh is not that far away. They could have come over easily by car or train or even on the bus."

"Yes, but according to the social media, both siblings have fairly intense schedules."

"Yeah, but doing what? Mostly just standing around."

"Attending parties, openings, dedications, all that stuff that occupy the life of the rich and famous."

"So what?"

Ron looked at his partner and said, "So, if they are present and in the public eye on many days, it reduces the days we need to look for their travel."

"Remember, they could've hired this out."

"Unless they did that. I don't want to think about that unless we stumble on a $25-50,000 cash withdrawal somewhere."

"What's the travel time to and from Pittsburgh?

"Item number one to determine," Ron said making a note.

By mid-morning they had developed a new framework for their review. Suspicion was heightened when they learned that the siblings were slow walking the probate. Sharon had added this gem from her own review of matters before going to the judge to request the warrant. It may have been the very tidbit that tipped the scales.

The detectives were operating on a strong assumption that someone in the family, or possibly more than one, was responsible for the three attempts and a final successful ending of Eugene's life. They also saw their biggest hurdle being the riddle of how one or more of the family got from Pittsburgh to Cincinnati and back without being missed at home or recognized in Ohio and done so without leaving a trail. In less than 30 minutes they were able to find costs and schedules for flights, busses and travel time between Pittsburgh and Cincinnati.

"If it were me, I'd just drive," said Gene. "It's only about five hours. And that would give me flexibility to leave when I wanted."

"I think I agree. Flights are going to restrict any quick exit. The bus traffic is sorta the same. Plus, it would take a whole day to get here by bus-and the same back to Pittsburgh."

"And look at the train schedule! It's like my daddy used to say, 'you can't get there from here. You have to go somewhere else first.'"

"If it's really the Cookes behind all this then, we oughta find a trail. Likely not tickets on public trans but gas receipts or food stops on the way."

"And the way most likely for someone to take is just following the Interstate to Columbus and then on down here."

"All right then, let's hit the records."

By late-afternoon they had become convinced that the evidence they were seeking was not to be found in the records they had.

"There is just nothing here," Gene said closing the last folder.

"I agree there's no smoking gun."

"Did you find anything in those ATM records?

"Not sure. I did notice that a day or two before every attempt on Eugene, Hamilton withdrew $200-250. Maybe he just did everything in cash."

"Any other such withdrawals?"

"Unfortunately, yes. There are three other similar withdrawals that don't pair up to anything here in Cincinnati."

"That's a hole in our case. Some smart defense attorney would use that information."

"Yeah, it definitely is a weakness. But if he's smart enough to keep from using his credit cards, maybe he was smart enough to cover up these withdrawals, too."

"Well, this really leaves us out of luck on the 'means' and 'opportunity' bases for our case. The judge may have been right." Gene slumped in his chair as he said this.

"I'm still thinking the siblings are the doers. They have the greatest motive. No one else has any kind of motive as far as we know."

"What about some family member of those guys that died in Nam? Maybe they found out who he was."

"Seems pretty far-fetched to me. He carried no identification and was completely mum about his name. How would they have ever figured out who he was? I think he was running so far and hard away from that time that he would not want anyone to know about it."

"Still, we have no other threads to pull on."

"Why else would the sibs be slow-rolling the probate? They really need to have Eugene declared dead. Why not just appeal to the court to make that declaration? It's been nearly fifty years."

"I don't know. Maybe they're worried that he could still show up. Especially now that there's newspaper coverage of millions of dollars available in a will."

"OK. But, think about this. Let's say Eugene dies in an alley in Cincinnati. From any cause. What happens next? Body goes to the coroner. For any of these three attempts the coroner would say something like, 'alcohol poisoning' or 'drug overdose' or even 'natural causes'. No suspicion and no investigation."

Gene shook his head slowly before saying, "That might work out but how does that help them? I mean, they know he's dead but they can hardly bring that evidence to court, can they?"

"Wouldn't have to. All they have to do is wait for the coroner to check Eugene's fingerprints against the Department of Defense database and 'Surprise!' the long-lost brother is found!"

"And found dead."

"Right. And suddenly the whole will and probate activity would be much simpler."

"But he didn't have any fingerprints."

"They didn't know that."

Both men sat quietly for a few minutes thinking about the implications of the minimum information they had so far. Finally Ron spoke up, "I imagine he used the cash to buy the whiskey and probably even the heroin. Might have gotten them in Pittsburgh. That'll be hard to trace."

"And where did he get the SUX stuff?" asked Gene. "Tom says that's a medical thing, not something on the street."

"My brain is hurting. I say we stop and think about it tonight and start over in the morning looking for some other patterns in the money. We didn't see the big expenditure but maybe there's a pattern we just haven't seen yet."

"Yeah, OK. Maybe you need some J.J. and John." Gene commented, picking up his jacket. He was referring to Ron's habit of getting great insight into a case after an evening listening to jazz, hence the reference to J.J. Johnson and John Coltrane.

"Even they have to have something to work with,' Ron rationalized.

*   *   *

The next day was more of the same. They switched record types and reviewed each other's work from the previous day without finding anything useful. After two trips for coffee they were back sitting at their desks when Captain Thorason appeared, "Anything?"

"Nary a thing," Ron said, looking up without a smile. "We've got some cash withdrawals around the time of the attacks but no way to trace movement from Pittsburgh to Cincinnati. We think he drove."

"Huh." A decent pause then, "What you gonna do?"

'Not sure, Cap'n, but a great man once said, ' When you're looking for something, it always turns out to be in the last place you look'. And I'm coming to think that we need to be looking at these people directly."

"Huh."

"I think we should do what they have expected somebody to do all along." Ron said, sitting up straight in his chair and winking at Gene. "I'm going to ask Tom to call them with the bad news that their brother is dead."

Thor started toward his office but turned and said, "The reason things are in the last place you look is because you stop looking when you find 'em."

CHAPTER 50

Sunday, April 19

Ron was not surprised that Meg had made all the arrangements and told him that Sunday night was 'fried chicken' night. Somehow Meg seemed to know when Ron needed the comfort of his favorite meal, his best recordings of jazz players and a quiet evening of reflection. Well before he had met Meg, Ron had spent evenings in a small bar in the German town of Kaiserslautern, nursing a couple of beers and pondering cases he had been assigned. When he became aware of the surprising insight he seemed to have gained overnight, this musing while listening to jazz became a habit.

Gene called it his 'partnering with J.J. and John' referring to J.J. Johnson and John Coltrane. He had enough respect for the tradition that he sometimes tried to get Ron to invoke the habit as if it were a mystical power. Over the years in Cincinnati, however, Ron had rarely made the conscious decision to ask Meg for the fried chicken dinner. He had done that once and the mystical force had not been helpful for him with a very personal issue. Ron had concluded that the trigger for Meg to create the atmosphere was part of the experience and he just decided to wait for things to happen naturally. The key to that happening appeared to be a sensitivity of Meg's to discern when Ron was sufficiently puzzled by a case that he needed "J.J. and John'. And that was the right time to put other things down and shop for chicken parts.

Meg had not been attuned to cooking a fried chicken meal when she married Ron but had learned the craft from her mother-in-law. Surprised at the science that was involved in putting chicken parts rolled in flour into hot grease, Meg had some trouble initially in producing this 'comfort food' for Ron. She persisted, however, and for the past several years Ron had looked up from her fried chicken to declare, "Better'n Momma's."

The chicken, correctly rolled, fried and drained, was only part of the experience, of course. The Looneys had developed an entire arrangement of dishes and experiences around 'the meal'. There had to be mashed potatoes with a gob of butter in the middle of a pile. And green beans, of course. And cornbread made just right: stoneground cornmeal cooked in an iron skillet well greased with bacon drippings. Home-cooked Arkansas food-and the comfort it afforded its disciples-travelled well.

The Looneys also had developed a ritual around the entire meal. Ron stayed away from the kitchen while it was being prepared but when the meal was over, he would take the dishes to the sink and rinse them. Meg would then open the oven to disclose a freshly baked apple pie. Ron's piece of pie was served with a large slice of cheddar cheese, a habit more common in New England than the South. Ron's family had always taken cheese with their apple pie and he once explained that it seemed to be a tradition in the dairy country where his father had grown up.

Meg had originally thought it strange to put cheese on pie, preferring ice cream herself. She once went to the local library and researched the practice finding to her surprise that it wasn't a new fad. Apparently as far back as the 14th century, English people either served cheese as a dessert or combined the cheese with some sweet pastry. In the American colonies of Britain long before any revolution was considered, apple pie covered in cheese was well rooted in the culture.

She brought Ron a big slice of pie with the cheese partially melted on it and a cup of coffee. He smiled and signed, "You know I want to have this served at my funeral." Meg had heard this before and responded, "Just the pie? Or the chicken, too?"

"The whole meal, honey. I'm personally convinced that if I have an open-casket funeral, the aroma from this food would wake me up."

"I probably should get a patent on that, then," she said sitting down with her pie.

Later, Ron took the dishes to the sink and they stood next to each other, washing and drying the dishes. Sometime during this part of the evening, Ron began to think about what he was going to do with the case and he tended to be withdrawn and less communicative. When the dishes were sitting in the drying rack they sat at the table once again sipping a fresh cup of coffee.

"Did you go to the library?" he asked.

"Went yesterday. I found a Tony Hillerman novel I haven't read." Meg's habit was to give Ron the whole downstairs for his ruminations while she took a new book upstairs and read in bed. After a last swallow, she got up, took her cup to the sink to rinse it out. She kissed him on the top of his head as she left for upstairs. "Goodnight, honey"

"Goodnight."

Shortly, Ron walked into the living room with another cup of coffee and turned his attention to the record player. It was basically an old turntable attached to Looney's home system: built-in pre-amplifier connected to two 15-inch speakers. He searched through his collection and selected a classic album, *Kind of Blue*, to start the evening and he set another album, *Saxophone Colossus*, aside to follow. He thought the soft thrumming of Paul Chambers' bass and the haunting notes from Miles Davis would fit his initial reverie. But he also recognized the risk of his falling asleep to Davis' treatment and set out the Sonny Rollins tracks to keep that from happening. He adjusted the volume to a low setting so the sound wouldn't keep Meg awake.

Then he began his routine. He arranged the information he had in the best chronological order as they understood. His earliest entry was a copy of the discharge summary from Eugene's admission in early November of last year. He had made some penciled notes on the discharge summary after talking with Ben Nealy. He laid out the sheets of information he had collected as well as all his notes and the copies of financials collected via the warrant. Once again he looked for the 'how' his primary suspects, Eugene's known brother, Hamilton, or sister, Penelope, would have been able to get from Pittsburgh to Cincinnati and back. Finished with his coffee, he went to the refrigerator and got a beer, opened it and sat on the couch

Throughout the evening and into the small hours of the morning, Ron read, then re-read his notes and the discharge summaries. He had created a folder on every person involved in the case and he re-read those, as well. He realized he was getting sleepy and he picked an album by Anthony Braxton and Joe Fonda he knew would keep him awake. But after his third beer he still had gained no clarity at all on how the murderer got nearly 300 miles without leaving a smidgeon of evidence.

The access to the whiskey and the drugs he knew would be a waste of time to pursue. Whoever this person was, he or she operated on a cash basis and was, to that extent, untraceable. Ron put his head back against the couch and thought how easily he and Gene had handled the shotgun murder. Why wouldn't every murderer be that helpful and inattentive to details? As the poignant bass sounds lulled him to sleep he thought, "Why can't I figure out 'How' this guy got here?'

A few hours later he awoke for a call of nature and when he returned to the living room, Ron realized he was no longer was puzzled by 'How' because he realized he knew how to prove 'Who' was involved in Eugene's murder. He slept on the couch comfortably for the rest of the night.

CHAPTER 51

Monday, April 20

Ron called Gene well before seven the next morning.

"You up, partner?"

"Yes. If you want to call and wake me, you have to call much earlier than this," Gene retorted.

"I'm on my way to the Evidence locker. Meet me there."

"What's up?"

"If I'm right we got the bastard," Ron said disconnecting.

*   *   *

Thirty minutes later, they held the plastic bag with the discarded cap and gown that Ron and Tom had found on the staircase right after Eugene's death. "You think we can get touch DNA from this?" Gene asked.

"That's not a certainty, but that's not what I'm counting on," Ron answered as he pulled on gloves and carefully unrolled the gown. Inside he found what was looking for, the nitrile gloves worn by the man in the gown.

"You remember Thor telling us last year about the new technology where one of the technicians got fingerprints off the inside of some gloves?"

"I don't remember that," Gene said questioningly.

"Well, I do and we got the gloves that the murderer wore to kill Eugene. And we'll have his fingerprints on a card in a couple of hours."

"But we don't have anything to compare them to, do we?" Gene asked, brightening at the prospect.

"Not yet. But I've got a plan for that," Ron said as they headed for the lab.

*   *   *

Just before eight o'clock, Tom's phone rang as he was driving to work.

"Hello."

"It's Ron. I got an idea and I need some help from you."

"Always there to help Cincinnati's finest."

"What time will the Cookes arrive?"

"Late morning. They said they would drive over."

"That's good. Here's what I need you to do for me … "

*   *   *

It was actually early afternoon when the Cooke's finally arrived at New City. Their limousine pulled up in front and a liveried driver hopped out to open their door and assist them exiting the vehicle. The man was nearly six feet tall, erect and commanding in presence with thick greying hair. The woman was smaller, about five and half feet, dressed in a light colored suit and wearing a narrow brimmed hat on her dyed blond hair. Their entrance created a minor stir in the lobby; Beverly was there to greet them and to usher them into the executive suite.

Tom was standing outside the door to his office to greet them.

"I'm Tom Bolling, chief of staff. I'm sorry for your loss."

"Hamilton Cooke," said the fiftyish man. "You're the one that called us."

"That's right," said Tom.

"This is my sister, Penelope."

"Ms. Cooke," said Tom extending his hand.

"Actually, it's Mrs. Haines," she said softly.

"I'm sorry for your loss."

Hamilton tried to take control of the situation. "Can we see him now?" He was about Tom's height with very upright bearing and a way of speaking that gave everyone around him the impression that he was in charge.

"Well," Tom said, "very soon but there's the usual paperwork first." He motioned to Mary and she rose from behind her desk and said, "I'm Mary Brighthouse, Dr. Bolling's secretary. If you would just fill out these simple forms everything can get underway." She the handed each of them a clipboard with one sheet of paper.

"What's this?" asked Hamilton as he took the clipboard.

"Just do it, Ham," said Penelope taking the other clipboard.

"This is simply your statement attesting that you are who you say you are and that you have a familial relationship to the deceased before we go view the body," Mary said somewhat officiously.

"Protocol," said Beverly. "HIPAA requirements limit this kind of visitation to next-of-kin."

Both Cookes read and signed their respective papers and, at Mary's indication laid the clipboards on her desk.

Tom said, "That's done and we can now move on." He started for the door and everyone trailed after him, Beverly bringing up the rear.

As soon as they left the carpeted area of the executive suite, Tom was aware of a faint squeaking sound. Without making it obvious he indicated that Beverly should lead and he dropped back to talk to Penelope.

"How long has it been since you last saw your brother?" he asked while carefully watching Hamilton's strides.

"We never met him. He disappeared when his mother died and we were both born years later. We have heard a lot about him, of course, but never actually saw him."

"I did not know that," Tom lied.

"But I brought some of the pictures that Father always kept around. Eugene was his favorite, first son and all that."

By then Tom was certain; the squeaking was related to Hamilton's shoes. He nodded to Penelope absentmindedly as he had a flashback of the man pushing the food cart with what he thought was a squeaky wheel. Then something else flashed in his mind. He remembered the other thing about the food service worker that had struck him as odd but that had slipped his mind. The guy had been wearing dress shoes, not sneakers like all the other workers!

He took a deep breath and said, "Let me get the elevators," as he moved to the front of the group and pressed the down button.

They stood quietly in the elevator car, Tom staring straight ahead, thinking, 'It's him. I know it and I need to tell Ron.' In the basement they exited the elevator turned right and Beverly led them down the hall and into the morgue area.

Monique had arranged her area for the showing. All her technicians were out of the room; the body of Eugene was covered by a sheet and lying on a table close to the door. She stood by the head and, when everyone was arranged around the other side of the table she looked at Tom for a signal.

When he nodded, Monique drew back the sheet from Eugene's head and looked at the brother and sister for recognition. There was none. Penelope pulled the old photographs from her purse and handed them to Hamilton. He looked at them and then at Eugene. "It's fifty years difference," he said. "It's hard to say. But it does look like it could be him."

"But you have fingerprint proof, right?" asked Penelope.

"We are definitely certain that this man is Eugene Cooke," Tom agreed.

"That will be good enough for us," said Hamilton, as he turned toward the door. "What else do we have to do here?"

"I presume you had a chance to make some arrangements in Pittsburgh," Tom said.

"Yes. We chose the funeral home that cared for Father," Hamilton replied. He stepped away from the body and turned toward the door, signaling that he considered his work in the area was finished.

"Well, why don't we go back to my office and have some coffee while we fill out those transfer papers?" Tom was having some difficulty continuing to be polite to this man and he hoped it wasn't showing.

"All right," said Hamilton taking his sister's arm and starting for the door. Beverly opened the door and behind their back looked inquiringly at Tom. He shrugged and they all started back for the elevator. The walk down the hall and the subsequent elevator ride was singularly silent.

CHAPTER 52

Monday, April 20

This time Mary met them at the door to the Executive suite and led them into the Director's Conference room. She had placed the necessary paperwork for transfer of remains on the table for them to examine and she had obtained a large pot of coffee. The Cookes sat at the table, Penelope hardly paying attention to the papers, Hamilton quickly reviewing them preparatory to signing. Mary distracted them both for a few minutes as she fussed over their coffee. "Cream?" she asked. Then, "Sugar?" before putting a napkin and cup in front of each. The cup she set in front of Hamilton was placed right on top of the papers he was reading.

Tom and Beverly also were handed cups with a good deal of fanfare about the need for cream or sugar as if Mary had no idea what they took in their coffee.

Several minutes later Hamilton drank the last of his coffee, shoved the cup aside, reached inside his jacket and pulled out a pen to finish filling out the transfer papers. He checked his phone for the correct address and telephone number for the funeral home in Pittsburgh. Finished, he shoved the paper toward the center of the table and asked, "Will there be a death certificate?"

"Of course," Tom replied. "It has already been completed."

"I'd like a copy of that, if I may," Hamilton said.

Tom was about to answer that request but at that moment, the door from the office area opened to allow entry to Ron and Gene.

"Come in, gentlemen," Tom said, relieved at their presence. "Hamilton, I'd like you to meet Ron Looney and Gene Novalchek."

Hamilton also rose to his feet and extended his hand, "Hamilton Cooke," he said. "And what is your role here?"

Ron said, "Pretty straightforward, Mr. Cooke. We are the arresting officers."

Everyone in the room took a deep breath and as Hamilton Cooke was about to speak, Ron interrupted him, "Hamilton Cooke you are under arrest for the murder of your brother, Eugene Cooke. Turn around and put your hands behind you. You have the right to remain silent. Anything you say can and will be used against you in a court of law. You have the right to an attorney. If you cannot afford an attorney, one will be provided for you. Do you understand what I just said?"

"What the hell … ," started Hamilton.

"Do you understand what I just said?" Ron interrupted tugging on the handcuffs he had placed on Hamilton.

"Yes, I understood you but what do you think you're pulling here?"

Ron did not reply but moved him toward the open doorway where two uniformed officers were waiting. They took Hamilton by the arms and led him out of the executive suite.

Penelope watched all this with wide eyes but silently. Then she stood and marched out of the room and left the office suite on her way through the lobby to her waiting limousine.

Tom started to tell Ron about the squeaking shoes but was interrupted by Gene saying, "That clipboard thing was a beauty. We not only got his prints off the clipboard but also on a sheet of paper saying what his name was. This should be a slam dunk!"

Beverly, who had not been aware of the events as thoroughly as Tom asked, "Where did you find prints involved in the murder?"

"Inside the gloves he used. The ones he left for us on the stairs."

CHAPTER 53

Friday, April 25

Tom asked Beverly to once again get the conference room available for a discussion with Ron and Gene. Ron had called and said he had a story to tell about the Cooke family involvement and Tom insisted that all relevant parties get a chance to hear the latest facts and fill in the background to the drama they had acted in unawares for many months.

He chose end of day for the meeting as much to reduce interference with regular workday activities as to be certain that the administrative offices were empty. Mary did her magic with the coffee pot and water bottles.

Monique was the first, other than Tom and Beverly, to arrive. She was not wearing her white coat and appeared ready to walk out the door on her way home for a spring weekend. Tom reflected that as he had felt harassed and put upon by the events of the Eugene Cooke saga, he could not recall that Monique ever looked anything other than fresh, engaged and professional. He was reminded how fortunate he was to have her at New City.

Ben Nealy arrived in a hurry and Tom thought 'this is a young man who seems always to be in a bit of a hurry.' Ben also was not wearing a white coat but he looked like his daily activity had just been put on 'pause' while he attended this meeting. Tom said, "Ben, get a cup of coffee and have a seat. You're going to like this."

Ben nodded but grabbed a bottle of water instead and sat next to Monique. He then pulled out his phone and began sending a text.

Ron and Gene were the last to arrive. Ron brought a large accordion folder, which he laid on the table while he went for the coffee pot. Gene looked around, smiled at everyone and also got a bottle of water.

Tom spoke first. "Ron has told me a little about the background to what the Cooke's involved us in over the last several months and I asked him to say what he can about it now that the investigation is closed. Monique is here to wrap up the autopsy and clinical findings. But first, I want to tell you what I have learned about Eugene Cooke to help you put these events into perspective."

"I don't have information about Eugene's early life or his upbringing and maybe Ron has more on that. What I do know is that this man, as a young man, left a home of moneyed privilege to enlist in the Army at the peak of military activity in Vietnam. There was a draft in place and many others with his financial capability were findings way to avoid military service but he chose to walk into a recruiting center and sign himself up."

Tom paused at that moment to allow the group to reflect back to that time, to remember the many forms of 'draft dodging' that occurred and think about the kind of person that would leave fortune to join the army in those days.

"It's not completely clear in the record but I suspect that as an enlistee he was given some latitude about choosing his Army path. While still in Basic Training, he distinguished himself sufficiently to be allowed to sign up for Ranger training."

"In that day, we had not the history of the Navy Seals or Army Rangers to admire. Those were the days to come. And our boy, Eugene Cooke, was determined to be one of those Special Operators."

Tom paused again to sip from his cup of coffee before returning to the tale. "I won't go through all the rigor of Ranger training. I suspect it's even harder than we can imagine. The day before he finished Ranger School Corporal E. Cooke was provided his first overseas orders. He was assigned to Vietnam, as expected, to be at Camp Minh Long, a base that was just spinning up for training of Vietnamese soldiers. His service record is scanty on events there for the first several months but the event I really want to call to your attention happened some six months later. Cpl. Cooke led an eight-man squad on a reconnaissance mission inland to determine Viet Cong strength along the highways. They had completed their assignment and were on the way back to base when they were ambushed. The squad lost two men in the initial attack and remained pinned down without relief. They spent three hours in a firefight with an unknown number of enemy combatants before they could be evacuated and lost two more men during that three hours. The remaining members of the squad later testified that they felt their position would have been overrun at the time of evacuation and that they all would have died except for the actions of Squad Leader Corporal Eugene Cooke. According to the testimony of his squad members, Cpl. Cooke took and held a defensive position that minimized the enemy's ability to fire on the evacuation area. This brave act allowed the others to evacuate before Cpl. Cooke left his post and ran through a field of fire to get to the helicopter."

Tom looked around the room and made eye contact with each individual. He could see that their opinion of the irascible old man they had seen and treated was undergoing a change.

"Cpl. Cooke was nominated for a Bronze Star. He refused to have the recommendation forwarded. The recommendation has a footnote quoting Cpl. Cooke as saying, 'no one should get rewarded for losing half of his men.' "

Tom paused again. "Subsequently, Cpl. Cooke was disciplined several times for fighting and drunkenness before he left the service at the end of his tour. And there is little known of his life or times from then until late last year."

"I think it is clear that Eugene did not cope with losing half his men on that mission. I believe it caused him grief and despair and anger. I have seen more than enough examples of this in my time in the military. Eugene lost his men and the army had no support for him and no way to help him get over the loss. I believe he felt not only responsible but unworthy and that led to depression and alcoholism and ultimately to an alley in the middle of the country."

"This story should help us each to understand a little more about Eugene Cooke. But probably only just a little. There's clearly more to the more recent story and I've asked Monique to tell us about the end.

CHAPTER 54

Friday, April 25

Monique did not move from her seat at the table. She nodded at Tom and spoke in her clear voice, "The autopsy results were very clear and distinct." The cause of death was air embolism of approximately 50 milliliters."

She paused and then continued, "Mr. Cooke also had extensive and severe cerebral atrophy, presumably related to a previous episode of respiratory failure as a consequence of being dosed with succinylcholine. In agreement with the pre-mortem EEG and neurological examination, I believe that Mr. Cooke would never have regained consciousness.

Again there was a slight pause in her presentation. "Other expected abnormalities included stage three cirrhosis of the liver with some degree of portal hypertension and an enlarged spleen as a result of significant alcohol intake over a protracted period of time."

Everyone in the room nodded; these findings were not a surprise any more than the cerebral anoxia.

"But perhaps the most significant finding," Monique said with only the slightest rise in her voice, "was the large gastric cancer found on the lesser curve of his stomach." Another pause. "And there were multiple metastatic lesions in his lungs, liver and thoracic spine." The sharp intake of air by nearly everyone in the room indicated to her that Tom had not revealed this finding prior to the meeting.

She continued, "And my estimation is that he would not have lived more than a few months before dying from this malignancy." That pronouncement was met by the now expected stunned silence. "To be clear," she explained, "if Hamilton Cooke had simply taken the time to get to know his brother, he would have known he didn't have to murder him; the old will would be irrelevant before the end of the year."

After allowing a few moments for reflection, Tom picked up the thread of presentation and turned to Ron.

"Ron?"

The detective sat forward in his chair at the table and said, "A lot of what we know came from some deep digging by Gene and me, some from things Tom and the two of you taught us." He indicated Monique and Ben. "And many of the final pieces really came to light only when Hamilton Cooke confessed."

"Did he act alone, then?" Asked Monique.

"Seems so," Ron answered and Gene nodded.

"How'd you get him to confess?" Beverly asked. "I thought he would lawyer up and batter away at 'coincidences'."

"He might have, but even his lawyer seemed to understand the weight of evidence we had from the gloves used by the person who injected the fatal air. When we got him to talking about how clever someone was to hide so many things from us and he started to brag."

"That doesn't sound like the police interrogations we see on television," Ben added.

"Well, you understand they only have an hour to solve the crime." Gene said. "In our world the clock never stops. A lot like baseball."

Ron went on, "Like I said, we got him to talking … "

"How did you do that?" asked Monique

"I played dumb," said Ron. "Just an old country policeman. Just couldn't figure out how he did certain things, like get here from Pittsburgh and not be missed. And he told me how dumb I really was and how easy it was to do those things."

"And that's all it took?" asked Beverly.

Gene interrupted, "You folks may not know this but Ron is excellent at playing dumb. I think it's his real second nature. Some people think it's his first."

After a brief laugh at his expense, Ron went on, "Gene and I have now put together a timeline that we will be presenting in court someday. Remember, Hamilton and Penelope never saw Eugene. He was out of the family life before they were born. Their mother let his father keep a few of his pictures around but she forbade much discussion about Eugene. He was just a mystery man to them. Off somewhere no one was sure where, possibly doing great and heroic things but again, no one actually knew.

"Then, sometime in the mid-1990s Hamilton got a severe sore throat and the old family doctor gave him some antibiotic that knocked out his bone marrow."

Monique said, "Probably chloramphenicol."

"Yeah," Ron said. "That sounds like it. Anyway he got very low sick and his doctors were then talking about he might need a bone marrow transplant. Penelope was not a good match and so Ham and the father hired a private detective to find Eugene. Took him several months to do so and while he was searching around, 'Lo and Behold' Hamilton's bone marrow recovered."

Everyone looked at Monique as if she had caused this miraculous turn of events. "Not so surprising, actually," she explained. "Chloramphenicol causes suppression of the bone marrow while it is being administered and that sometimes looks permanent. The real damage is if the marrow quits a few months after the treatment. That type of damage does not recover."

Ron nodded, "Hamilton said his doctors told him something like that. They thought this was permanent but it wasn't. And, as he was recovering without the transplant, the PI showed up with the news that he had found Eugene. Hamilton took the information and kept it from his father. He knew more than twenty years ago that Eugene was a bum on the streets of Cincinnati.

"That explains the short time between the news of the will that excluded Hamilton and the first attack on Eugene, I guess," said Tom.

"That's the way we look at it too," Ron continued. "When the father died and the lawyer told Hamilton about the strange will, they had a discussion about the best way to handle the problem. All things said and done, the best solution was for a death certificate for Eugene to turn up. Then the lawyer would declare the father had died intestate and the Pennsylvania probate process would divvy up the estate between the two living children."

"What did Penelope know of all this?" asked Beverly. "She looked completely at sea when he was arrested."

"According to him, she knew nothing of his plan. He didn't really trust anyone, I guess. And if he had only thrown his gown and gloves into a hopper with all the others we never would have caught him."

"But how did he actually do it? Get at 'Barry', I mean, Eugene?" Ben wanted to know.

"Quite easily, according to Hamilton. He bought the whiskey-and later the heroin-in Pittsburgh. He would leave the city and drive to Cincinnati early in the morning so he could be here before noon. He had a picture of Eugene from the PI and he hunted around the areas where the homeless congregate until he found him. Then he just struck up a conversation and gave him the bottle. Naturally, he thought that would be it. He drove home and watched the paper for a few days without seeing any obituary or getting a call. He thought that Eugene's fingerprints would show up in the DoD database and he'd get the needed death certificate.

"So he came back, this time with heroin. Got Eugene to take a sleeping pill and then injected the needle. Hamilton said he almost got caught that time because the police were checking on the homeless that night and Eugene yelled when he stuck him. When he still didn't get a call he got to thinking about how to be certain that the guy was dead so he couldn't be saved. You had really ruined his life up to that point, Ben."

Ben smiled wryly but had nothing to say.

Gene picked up the story, "Hamilton had been around when his father died and remembered that the nurse had a ventilator brought into the house in case he couldn't breathe. His father did not want to end up on a machine and refused to use it. The nurse had told Hamilton that she had some medicine-a paralytic she called it-that would allow her to put in the breathing tube on a moment's notice. Apparently she wanted to assure Hamilton that if his father did end up on the ventilator it would be easy on him. At this point Hamilton remembered they had stored several medications in his father's bedroom during the last few months of his life. He searched the area and found a small vial of succinylcholine. Did I say that right, doctors?"

Tom and Monique nodded and Tom indicated that Gene should continue.

"Somewhere he got another syringe like he had with the heroin and made still another trip. This time he thought he'd better sneak up on Eugene who just might remember the bad things that happened to him the last time Hamilton had shown up. He filled the syringe and hung around, when it looked like Eugene was asleep he walked past and injected him in the butt and kept walking. Eugene woke up and started hollering and police came and you know the rest."

Ben said, "That explains something I didn't understand."

"What's that? Tom asked.

"I don't know what size bottle of SUX he had, but if he just had a heroin needle he didn't use enough to kill him. I wondered why he had gotten just a partial dose."

"What about the attack in the hospital?" Tom interjected. "Was it like I said?"

Ron picked up the story, "Actually it was almost exactly that way. He found out that Eugene was here in New City and he just walked in and read the signage. He found the doctors' dressing room and gowned up. After putting on a cap and mask he walked the halls until he found the right ward He found an empty food tray cart against a wall so he started pushing it around and looking in rooms until he found his brother."

"And the syringe? What about that?" Tom wanted to know.

Ron nodded, "I know that bothered you. Hamilton said it was right there in the room. He undid the intravenous line and squirted a bulb full of air and replaced the line and walked out just as the alarms went off."

"Yes. I know. I saw that."

"While the resuscitation was going on, Hamilton just walked to the elevators and decided to ditch the cart and take the stairs. He was back in Pittsburgh for dinner, ready to take the call about his poor brother's death."

There was a pause while everyone took a breath. They had just heard something that sounded like it belonged in a Hollywood movie. But it had actually happened right there in their own hospital literally right under their noses. They had each played a part in a story revolving around greed and 'murder most foul' as the Bard had put it.

"Ben," said Tom, "I consider this all your fault."

"Wh . . .What's that, sir?" Ben's head snapped around.

"Catching a murderer who would have gotten away with it if you hadn't been so clever."

"Acknowledgements"

I want to thank my wife and children for their encouragement during this writing process. Their feedback, support, and encouragement were positive factors in me finishing the original manuscript.

I also want to recognize Elle Murray for her faithful and frequent efforts to clean up the manuscript and to assist me in getting to the right place in decisions about format, artistry, and pagination.

Any errors that escaped these screening activities are mine alone.

Galen Barbour

Alexandria, Virginia

January 2023

Interested in another G.L. Barbour
Medical Murder Mystery?

During the summer of inner-city riots, Cincinnati's downtown unease causes manpower shortages in homicide and for the Drug Task Force. The Task Force is struggling with a fentanyl overdose wave and Ron Looney and Gene Novalchek have their hands full with the murder of a young woman on the college campus. The two investigations ultimately overlap and require Tom Bolling, chief of staff at New City, to use his understanding of medical administrative oversight to begin the unraveling.

Excerpt

The apartment was small, almost cozy. A one-bedroom place, it had matching tiny living area and an eat-in kitchen. The presence of the four men seated around the table seemed to occupy most of the space available. One of the men was older, looked nearly sixty, and had brown hair streaked with broad-brush strokes of yellowish gray. He wore half-glasses perched on a broad and bulbous nose and the eyes behind the frames were small and sharp. He directed a question at the man across the table from him, "This place is good for how long?"

"No mor'n a week," said the man. He was thin and wiry with a rather plain face; his eyes did not actually look at the questioner but generally in his direction. He wore an over-sized V-neck sweater with sleeves pushed up and which kept falling down.

"Then we need a new place for next week," said the older man, clearly the leader of the group. He looked at the men to each side and they nodded.

"I think I'll have a place by then," said the man on the right. He was a large man, close to 300 pounds wearing a sweat stained undershirt. He had a shaved head glistening with sweat and multiple tattoos visible on his large, bare arms. "Looks like the place next door to me is gonna open up in the next day or so."

Satisfied, the leader turned his attention back to the several stacks of money on the table. In front of him was a clipboard to use for tallies. The other three were counting the money, bundling packets of $1000 and stacking them for his tally. The tabletop held several loose bills and three handguns. The men did their work in silence.

Suddenly, there was a bump at the door and it opened to admit a young woman. Her presence so startled the men that two of them had grabbed their weapons before realizing the absence of any threat. She was carrying a pizza box and a wide-eyed stare that took in the money and the guns.

"Peg," said the wiry man as he stood and positioned himself between the girl and the table. "What're you going here?"

"Ummm. I thought we could watch a movie?" she said hesitatingly.

"I probably should have told you we'd do that some other time," he said starting to move her toward the door.

Behind him the leader had swept most of the money into a duffel bag. He stood and noted that the weapons were concealed. "Look, TJ, we have pretty much finished the count. Don't let us interrupt your date," he said with a light inflection on the idea of a 'date'.

The man called TJ turned questioningly toward the leader who explained, "All we have left to do is to justify the last of these receipts and we'll be outta your hair. Why don't you and the lady go on and watch your movie?" He indicated with his head in the direction of the bedroom where the only television was kept. "I'm sorry we ran over so late."

TJ took the hint and smiled at the girl, "Sure. Good idea." He led her toward the bedroom and locked eyes with the leader as he passed.

9 798893 565157